S. Fannie Gerry Wilder

Boston Girls at Home and Abroad

S. Fannie Gerry Wilder

Boston Girls at Home and Abroad

ISBN/EAN: 9783337419844

Printed in Europe, USA, Canada, Australia, Japan

Cover: Foto ©Andreas Hilbeck / pixelio.de

More available books at **www.hansebooks.com**

BOSTON GIRLS

AT HOME AND ABROAD

BY

S. FANNIE GERRY WILDER

AUTHOR OF "THE STORY OF A USEFUL LIFE."

"Not by appointment do we meet Delight and Joy;
They heed not our expectancy,
But 'round some corner in the streets of Life
They spring and clasp us with a smile."
— GERALD MASSEY.

BOSTON:
JAMES H. EARLE, PUBLISHER,
178 WASHINGTON STREET.
1890.

To All Young People,

WHO WILL ENJOY SPENDING AN HOUR IN SCHOOL
AND AT HOME WITH THE YOUNG FRIENDS
WHO LIVE IN THESE PAGES,

This Story is Dedicated,

BY THE AUTHOR.

CONTENTS.

VIII.

IX.

X.

XI.

XII.

BOSTON GIRLS

AT HOME AND ABROAD.

I.

THE NEW FRIENDS.

OME, children, you must hurry, or you will be late for school," said Aunt Fannie, as she looked at the French clock, which was ticking away on the mantelpiece, its hands pointing to ten minutes of nine o'clock.

"Oh, auntie," said Mary, "that clock must be fast."

"I think not, but *you* are very slow. I am afraid you are two very sleepy children in the morning. You must 'turn over a new leaf,' and have for your motto, 'Early to bed and early to rise, makes a man (boy or girl) healthy, wealthy, and wise.'"

So saying, she helped Mary tie her hat, and put on Hugh's coat.

Kissing tne children, she stood watching them as they disappeared over the hill. *Other* eyes saw the little figures run down the hill and turn the corner on their way to school.

"I wonder who those children are," thought Mrs. Grey; "they are always in a hurry; such pretty children, too! What lovely golden curls the little girl has! She looks like a fairy flitting along, with her ringlets floating in the breeze."

It was a beautiful morning in the early part of September, the sun shining so brightly, the sky so blue, with the warm wind, "just like summer, it was almost too fine to think of study," so said the children; but they ran along, looked at the church clock, saw it was nearly five minutes of nine, hurried even more, and arrived nearly breathless at the school door. Hugh must go still farther, so kept up his speed, but, alas! was late. Mary was just in time, but as she sank, all out of breath, into her seat, she resolved to follow Aunt Fannie's advice of "Early to bed and early to rise." However, the good resolution was so very hard to keep and carry out, that almost every morning the same thing was repeated.

As nine o'clock struck, the bell called the children to order, and the morning work began in the various classes. As it was the very first week of school, after the long vacation, the scholars were hardly in working order. Miss French, who was the teacher in the room where little Mary Swan—for that was her name—was placed, gave them some examples in arithmetic to do, while she was busy in other ways. As they were thus employed, the master of the school opened the door, followed by two ladies and two little girls who both looked rather frightened. They were pretty little girls; one with sandy hair, blue eyes, a sweet little mouth, and a fair complexion, and the other with a chubby, round face, red cheeks, and brown hair. Evidently no relation to each other, in fact strangers until then

" Here are two new scholars for you, Miss French; I think they are suited for your class," said Mr. Babcock.

" I think this lady will be just the right person to take charge of your little girls," he said to the ladies.

Miss French took the children by the hand, drew them to her, saying, " Now, tell me your names, for I want to put them in my big book."

The blue-eyed stranger hung her head and began to cry, but the rosy-cheeked one answered promptly, "My name is Etta Kendall, and I am ten years old."

"Now what is your name, my dear?"

"Frances Grey, and I am ten years old," whispered the other little girl.

"Well, here are two seats, side by side, you may have, and I know you are going to be the best of friends and very happy with all these children."

The other scholars, who had been attending more to the strangers than to their own work, looked very wise. Mary, with her bright eyes full of fun, whispered to Annie, "that it was silly to cry, and she would n't do so any way."

The teacher said, "Now, children, how many have the examples done?" She looked in vain for one single hand raised in answer.

"I think you must have been very busy watching the new scholars. Mary, I thought you always liked to get your done first."

Mary hung her head, as she knew she had not been quite faithful — rather of an "eye servant."

"Now close your books, fold your arms, and

give me your attention. Take 3+3+3+1, how many?"

"Ten!" said Mary.

"Take 10−2−2−3−2−1?"

"Zero!" said Kitty.

Just at this moment the gong struck for recess. How the bright eyes sparkled at the prospect of a run into the fresh air! The teacher opened the door, and the children filed down the stairs very quietly, but when the school-yard was reached, what a noise they made, shouting and calling, as they ran about the yard; playing "tag," "hide-and-seek," and "I spy"!

Mary, Kitty, and Annie, who had stopped to take breath, saw the little strangers standing together, looking with wonder at the game of romps, feeling very forlorn.

"Let us ask them to play," said Kitty. "All right," answered Mary; and they ran up to the girls.

"Come and play tag with us."

"Let me take hold of your hand," said Mary to little Frances.

Annie took Etta by the hand also, and in a few minutes they were running around and shouting with the rest of the children, as happy as they could be. Yes; Miss French had truly said "that they would have a good time with the other little girls."

"I like them ever so much," said Kitty, as they went back into the school-room.

When all was quiet, the teacher had them sing a number of pretty songs, and then take their reading books. An hour was pleasantly spent, then hardly before they knew it, twelve o'clock came. So each day passed, every hour being devoted to some duty, the little ones learning many valuable lessons which would help them as they grew older.

These young girls, who were schoolmates and friends, were all living in the city of Boston, Mass., and were very fortunate children, for they had many blessings, — kind parents and pleasant homes.

Mary Swan had lost her dear mother, who had been called away from her family and was "safe in heaven," so Mary said, as she spoke of her "dearest mamma," whose pictured face looked down from above the mantel, beaming with youth and beauty, upon her children; the eyes seemed to tell of her love for them, and of the blessings she would shower down upon them.

Mary's father was a doctor, a very busy man, indulgent in every way to his children; and with Brother Hugh, two years younger, Sister Sarah, who was a grown-up young lady, "dear Aunt Fannie," and "blessed old Grandpa," — a very happy home this little girl possessed. Their house was situated in a very pleasant part of the city, so near the beautiful Common that the children and their friends could have this spot for their play-ground.

Kitty Lee and Annie Bell were born in Boston, Frances Grey and Etta Kendall were born "down East," but now had homes in this good old Puritan city. They had never known each other until that first day in school, but were ever afterwards the best of friends, through their girlhood and womanhood.

Mr. Grey, the father of Frances, was an earnest minister, who had come from a distant city to carry on the good work in Boston, and the family had only lived here for a few years. A very pleasant home was theirs, and Frances dearly loved her good father and mother, also her Brother Ed., who loved his little sister very much, but like all boys, delighted to tease her "just for fun," so he said.

Poor Etta, sad to say, was an orphan; she had

lost both parents suddenly; an aunt had taken the child to her home, and Etta was trying very hard to bear this grief.

Poor child! she was very lonely at times and often shed bitter tears as she thought of the pretty country town where she had lived, and of the lovely home in which all were so happy together. It is a sad thing for a child to lose either father or mother, but when both are gone it is a pitiful condition.

It seemed strange to go to a city school, but she told her aunt, "it was just splendid, and the girls were so nice." She often thought of the little school-house and the good teacher keeping guard over her flock. What fun it was at recess, to play hide-and-seek in the shady grove just opposite, and such a nice place for luncheon, in the "nooning" between school hours. Not very much like the city street, with its high brick walls and the orderly school-room, furnished so neatly for the comfort of the scholars.

Annie Bell was an only child, with an invalid mother, so that she must always be "as quiet as a mouse" at home, for her mamma was often very ill. Owing to this, she did so much enjoy having a good romp with the girls, laughing and shouting just as loud as she possibly could, but she was so fat she could not run very fast, and almost always was the last one to reach the "gool."

Kitty Lee was a tall, slender girl, with dark brown hair and bright blue eyes. Her numerous brothers and sisters filled the home-nest full, but there was always a nice, warm corner in it for Kitty. One could seldom see such a pretty group of girls together as they were, and many people often turned to look at them as they wended their way home from school, chattering just like magpies. As the children ran along from school, that noon, on their way home, they passed a baker's shop.

"Wait a minute, I am hungry," said Mary, as she disappeared through the door, coming out shortly with a paper bag in her hand, full of "goodies." They proved to be big buns, with currants in them, and she gave one to each of the girls, who thought "that buns were the nicest luncheon that they could have."

"Where do you live?" asked Mary of little Frances, as they turned the corner of Bow street.

"On this street, and in this house."

She stopped before the door of a pretty

brown-stone cottage, perched on top of the hill. It was a cosy-looking house, covered with wood-bine. Her mamma opened the door, as she spoke.

"Well, little girl, home so soon? How did you like school? Who is this little girl?"

"Mary Swan, she goes to my school, and she gave me a bun, see!" said Frances, holding up what was left of it.

"Can't your little girl come and play with me? I live a few steps from here, on Hill street."

"She must eat her dinner now, but to-night after school she can play with you."

"I have some pretty rabbits, and a darling little kitten, and my Brother Hugh has a cun-ning pony in our barn. You can see them *all*, if you will come."

"Oh! I will just as soon as I can," shouted Frances, as Mary ran up the hill towards home.

"What a lovely child," said mamma. "I have noticed her very often. I am glad you will have such a nice little girl to play with."

Frances could talk of nothing else all dinner time but the rabbits, the kitten, and the pony she was going to see after school. She told her father she wanted a pony, too.

"My dear little girl, where should we keep it? We have no barn, even if I was rich enough to buy a pony; but you can have a kitten, and we will ask Aunt Martha to give us one, when we go to see her next summer."

"I can't wait so long, I want one now! Can I write to Cousin May to send me one right off?"

"Yes," said papa, "she can send it in a box by express."

So Frances ran for her pen, ink, and paper, but she was so excited that she could n't spell the words right, so mamma wrote a note for her, and Frances dropped it into the letter-box, on her way to school that afternoon.

How long the two hours seemed to the girls, who were thinking more of the fun they should have after school was done, than of storing their minds with the useful facts in the geography lesson, which good Miss French was trying so hard to impress on their minds! The lesson was on the capitals and principal cities of the New England States. Poor little Frances tried very hard to remember whether Boston was in Massachusetts or Maine, but as it came her turn to point out the city on the map, her thoughts were so far away, thinking of the cunning rabbits and whether they would be black or white, that she pointed to the northern part of Vermont. Miss French looked sober, as so many of her best scholars made such blunders in the lesson, she didn't know what a splendid time they were looking foward to, or how the hours seemed to lag to their impatient spirits.

It was hot and close in the school-room; as the sun shone in, and the balmy breeze floated by, it made them long all the more for freedom to romp and play. At last the hours were gone, and they were free from the duties of school. They hurried as quickly as possible, stopping a moment to tell Mrs. Grey where Frances was going, and in a few moments were at the door of Mary's house.

"This is my home, come right in and see my Aunt Fannie."

They entered a large hall, which led into a pleasant parlor, with rooms opening on each side from it.

Aunt Fannie, a lovely-looking lady, sat sewing in the dining-room, and welcomed the little girls with a pleasant smile.

"We are going out to play in the barn. Where's Hugh?

"I think he is out there with Frankie Bliss, for I have heard a shouting in that direction since school, although I have not seen the boys," replied Aunt Fannie.

The girls hastened away, and soon were in the barn.

"Hugh, where are you? Come and help us up the ladder," called Mary.

A pretty boy appeared at the top of the ladder, which led into the loft above.

"Give me your hand, and I will pull you up," said he.

"This is Frances Grey, and you must help her first."

"All right; here goes!" shouted Hugh, as he pulled her, rather frightened, up into the loft.

The other girls, being more used to the ascent, were soon with her. Frances looked about, and in a few minutes spied the rabbits.

"Oh! you little darling," cried she as a white rabbit, with pink eyes, cuddled down into her lap and she stroked its soft back.

There was a whole colony of them of all sizes, black and white, "just lovely," said Frances.

The little girls petted them to their hearts' content, while the boys dashed around, throwing hay down to the horses.   Then how Hugh teased Charley, the man who took care of them, to saddle "Bobby," the pony!

"It is too late in the day, Master Hugh, but to-morrow afternoon you may take him out."

As it was getting dusk, Hugh had to be contented with the promise, but he was not very patient over it.

"Let us call 'Charley, barley,' to him," said he to the children.

So they sat down in the large window over the barn door and shouted, "Charley barley, wheat and rye, kissed the girls and made them cry! Oh! Charley!" This was not a kind thing for them to do, but he only laughed and whistled loudly.

"It is too bad to plague him, Hugh, he is so good to us, and papa would not like it, either. Come, girls, let us go into the house," said Mary.

"I can't come in to-night, but must go right home," said Frances.

So Kitty and Annie ran over the hill with her, and mamma was waiting at the door.   She chattered during tea-time about the "darling rabbits, the pony, and of the lovely fun it was to play with the cunning little things."

II.

FROM DAY TO DAY.

BOSTON COMMON is one of the most lovely spots in the city, — a source of pleasure to both young and old, rich and poor, — a resting-place for the fathers and mothers, and a play-ground for the children.

How lovely it is in the summer, with the green grass, tall trees, the nicely-kept paths (or malls, as they are called), branching off in all directions, the Frog Pond in the center, to vary the scene, and the sun shining over all, casting shadows here and there; then, in the winter, a fine place to coast down the steep paths, and skate on the ice.

Beyond the Common is the Public Garden, with its lovely flower-beds, fine statuary, and little lake, with a fanciful bridge crossing it, its waters covered by small pleasure boats. The children of Boston are very fortunate in having such a spot, that can be enjoyed by them at all times. On holidays, in the spring and summer, the grounds are covered with people, who come from all parts of the city, bringing their whole families with them and staying all day long, to enjoy this beautiful place. A great blessing it is to those who live in a crowded city.

These little friends lived so near the Common that they daily visited it, and felt as if it was a part of their home, so many happy hours were spent there. They went to school every day, learning to love the kind teacher who did so much for them, guiding their thoughts aright and instilling into their minds useful knowledge.

Little Frances was very happy in her new playmates and daily visited her friend, Mary Swan. The tiny rabbits grew to be quite large, and the children delighted to take them in their arms to the Common, put them on the grass, and let them hop about, taking care that they did not hop away too far.

On crisp autumn mornings Mary, Frances, and Hugh might be seen skipping down the broad mall; now resting on the seats, calling the gray squirrels, which lived on the Common, to take the nuts and crumbs of bread or cake from their hands. The little creatures were so tame that they would readily come to the call, and often disappear into the pockets of their coats. Then, how the children would laugh, as the little round heads, with their bright eyes, would pop out again, with a nut held tight in their paws!

One morning Aunt Clara—Mrs. Grey's sister—went with them to feed the squirrels. The knowing creatures came running towards them, and one brave fellow took a nut from Aunt Clara's hand. Turning as quick as a flash, it ran down the path to a certain tree—its home—to hide the nut, disappeared, then appeared, all in a moment. As it came back to beg another nut, a gentleman, resting on one of the seats near by, held out one to the squirrel. But the cunning fellow looked at him, smelt of the nut, and then ran to Aunt Clara, who also held one, seized it quickly and ran away, his black eyes twinkling with fun. How delighted the children were! They laughed and shouted, to think that "the midget should know auntie so well." The kind gentleman laughed, saying, "Well done, that was a cunning creature!"

At that time a row of noble elm trees lined Tremont street, from the Common to the Tremont House, and the space between each tree was occupied by a stand, upon which were displayed rosy-cheeked apples, peanuts, candy, and golden oranges. These sweets were watched over by such funny-looking little old women, who sat by the stands and sold their wares to passers-by. The children were always welcome, as they spent nearly *all* their bright pennies at these out-of-door stores. One old lady, who used to wear a pumpkin hood, little plaid shawl, and a large apron, was a great friend, and would say, " Here comes the darlints, bless 'em," as she took the cents in exchange for the peanuts.   Oftentimes the children would see the cunning squirrels run up to a peanut stand, beg the old lady who sold the "goodies" to give them one, and then whisk along the crowded streets into the granary burying-ground, where they would hide it for future use.

But, alas! the beautiful "Paddock elms" were in after years cut down, and the peanut stores, with the smiling tenders, were seen no more.

The boys would at times mark out the game of "hop scotch" on the broad Beacon-street mall, and what a jolly time they had, trying to kick the stone into the right square! The boys succeeded better than the girls, and always gained the best of the game, much to their delight.

Then the Frog Pond was such a nice place on which to sail the tiny boats, but the frail barques often tipped over, and would n't sail away, as the children wished them to.

Hugh would often say, "Come, girls, let 's ask Charley to saddle Bobby, and you may all have a ride. Now jump on, Frances."

"Oh, I am afraid!"

"You need n't be, I will hold you on," Charley would say, as he helped her to the pony's back and led him about the yard.

"Jump off now," Kitty would call, "I want a ride."

So all the children had a turn in riding the little creature, until Charley led him back to the barn. Thus the pleasant fall days flew by, and now the leaves began to cover the ground, and the bleak winds to blow, making every one think of the winter which was coming rapidly. Thick coats and dresses seemed comfortable, and the children were glad to stay indoors after school.

They began to feel that it was a great privilege, to be able to go to such a fine school and receive valuable instruction. The ambition to be good scholars, and take a high rank in the class, was felt, and the promise of a diploma, at the end of the school year, was something *real* to work for. But whether a reward of paper or silver was obtained, they would have the satisfaction of knowing that the knowledge could never be lost or taken away from any one, who did honest, careful study.

Mary Swan was a very bright scholar, and dearly loved arithmetic. She always had her examples right and could do them quickly; but for Frances it was very hard, and many times she gave up in despair, and shed bitter tears over her dulness. Multiplication examples were the very worst, and when, after great labor and careful study, the columns would not add up correctly, her vexation could hardly be controlled, and she often said, "it was no use, she could n't ever do them right."

Poor child! Her misery was increased by hearing the familiar strains of two hand-organs playing different tunes at the same time, just as she was trying so hard to multiply a long multiplicand by an equally long multiplier. "Annie Laurie" and "Home, Sweet Home," seemed to mix the figures all together, and she would have to put the lesson aside until another time.

"How I wish I could do examples as easy as Mary does," she often said to her mamma.

"Well, my dear child, if it is not so easy for you, then you will have to study all the harder; but patience and perseverance will accomplish wonders."

Frances did really envy her friend, and often felt that she was a most unfortunate girl, because this study of arithmetic was so hard for her. She was a very smart scholar in every thing else, delighting in history, and her compositions and reading lessons always received the highest rank. In fact, this group of girls was a bright circle, and the good teacher knew that they would always do their very best. They dearly loved to play, but they also liked to hold a high rank in school.

Thanksgiving Day had passed, and winter was rapidly approaching.

One morning, as Etta opened her eyes, she saw the snow-flakes falling fast.

"Oh, auntie, it is a regular Down-East snow-storm! Now for some fun! We can go coasting on the Common."

She was so impatient that she could hardly stop for breakfast, and ran as fast as she could to call for Kitty. As they started out for school, Annie hailed them, then Mary and Frances joined the group, and they all went skipping along, as merry as they could be over the prospect of a "good coast."

This was the first snow-storm of the season, and, as many followed, they had the wish fulfilled. The Common was covered deep with snow. A merry scene it was, as the coasters went over the smooth paths like lightning. The boys had their double-runners painted in gay colors, and, as one sled followed another, the course could hardly be seen, it was so covered by the various sleds of all sizes and every description. It was not a very safe place for the girls, so they kept on the side-paths and had just as good a time as the boys. It was also an entertaining sight for the older people to watch this sport, and many persons slackened their pace to see the happy youngsters at their play. It brought back to their minds the days of youth, and the enjoyment they themselves had in this very sport. What bright eyes and rosy cheeks this exertion gave these children, and they never thought of feeling cold! As the crowd of spectators watched them, many remembered, perhaps, the steep hills in New Hampshire, down which they used to coast, going so fast that sparks of fire seemed to be flying before them, until they reached the bottom of the hill in safety; then for a hard pull up, but they never minded that, as it was such fun to slide down again.

Walking to the Frog Pond, and over to the Public Garden, one could see the ice covered by groups of skaters, skimming along so easily. Mary and Kitty knew how to skate, but the other girls did not, much to their regret. When Frances was a very little girl, her idea of something nice to wear was a pair of *rubber boots.* She teased her mamma to buy them. "They look so nice," she said, and was proud enough when she became the owner of a shiny black pair of rubber boots. Now her great want was a *pair of skates.* When she made this known, her papa thought "she was rather a small girl to trust herself on such articles."

"Papa, I can learn to skate, I know, just as well as Mary does, if I only try."

She felt impatient because her papa did not gratify the wish at once.

"Christmas is coming," he would say.

Christmas was near at hand, and these friends were looking forward to a happy holiday. Every day Frances would tell "what she wanted the very most of any thing," and it was always the skates. The children saved up their pennies for a few weeks, after the peanut women found it too cold to keep store out-doors, and so had their very own money to spend. After school, they would go to the stores, which were gaily decorated and filled with beautiful and useful articles for Christmas.

Mary and Kitty disappeared mysteriously one day, and walked quickly over the hill to Tremont street. They entered a jeweller's store, and Mary asked for "silver thimbles."

"How large a size, miss?"

"I want one for a girl just about as big as I am."

"I think this will suit you."

"I want some letters put on it, so she will know who gave it to her. Can you say 'From Mary to Frances'?"

"I think, for such a small thimble, that will be too many words. You can have the initials engraved on it."

"Then please have 'M. E. S. to F. S. G.,' and I will call in a few days for it."

They made some other purchases, trying to get remembrances for all their little circle. As they were going home, whom should they meet but Etta and Frances, who quickly put a number of little bundles into their pockets.

"Have you been getting postage stamps?" said Kitty, with a laugh.

"We went to the office to see if they had some to-day, but did not get any new ones," replied Frances.

The girls had been collecting foreign postage stamps, and were very anxious to have a fine assortment. As they knew a number of places where foreign letters were received, they weekly visited these offices to obtain them.

"Come in, girls, and play Authors," said Mary, as they arrived at her door.

" I can come in for just a little while," replied Frances.

Kitty was willing to join the game, but Etta was doubtful, as her aunt did not like to have her stay away from home without permission. The temptation was too strong, as the game was a source of delight to all the girls.

They went into the dining-room, threw off their cloaks and hats. It was such a pleasant room, with a large bay-window overlooking the Common, and a bright fire burning in the grate made it look "so cosy," Frances said. They had played a number of games before it became dark, but still it was so delightful that they kept on, not realizing the time, until Norah, the girl, came in to light the gas and lay the table for tea.

Then Etta jumped up in a hurry. "What will aunt say? I know she will scold me for staying so long. I must go right home this very minute."

"Well, I will go along with you," added Kitty.

"I wish you both would stay to tea, for I know Frances can," replied Mary. "If you will stay, I'll have Hugh tell your mothers that you are all right. Then he can go home with Etta, and ask Charlie Williams to come and play with us. Can't you come back again, Etta?"

"I will if I can, but I am sure aunt will feel cross because I did n't come right home after school," she said.

As Hugh came in at that moment, Mary told him the plan.

"That's jolly! I will ask your aunt myself, and bring you back with me. Well, good-bye, until we see you again," shouted Hugh, as they trotted over the hill.

"I do hope she can come, but I know her aunt is so strict with her," said Kitty.

" We 'll play 'bear,' 'hide-and-seek,' and every thing for fun this evening," chatted Mary. " Let 's sit down before the fire and tell stories until they come."

They were now in the parlor, a lovely room, quite large, yet so comfortable. An open fire-place, filled with blazing wood, sent gleams of light over the room, making the lovely face of the dear mother, who had gone away and was waiting for her loved children in the heavenly home, "just like an angel's," said Mary, as she looked up to the pictured face.

The handsome carpet, heavy draperies, easy chairs, tables loaded with books, ornaments of every description, lovely pictures, and a fine piano, made up an apartment which was indeed beautiful.

It was a favorite resort of the children, and they thought that Mary's home was "a little bit lovelier than any other home could be."

" You tell a story, Kitty."

" I do n't believe I can."

" Oh! I know a cute one about my Brother Ed., when he was a little boy. Mamma told it to me the other day."

" Do tell us!" cried the girls; and they drew

up closer to Frances, who folded her hands in her lap and proceeded to tell the story.

"This is just what mamma said," she began. "I asked her to tell me something funny about big brother."

"'Well,' said mamma, 'once on a time, I had such a funny little boy. I loved him very much, but he was a great rogue. We did not live in the city then, but in a lovely country town.

"'All the people in the village knew my little boy, and thought he was very cunning, with his bright head and blue eyes. The children would say, 'What has sonny been doing to-day?' 'Oh!' I would say, 'he has been such a mischievous boy, I can hardly tell you.'

"'One day a great flock of sheep appeared in the shady road. A very good company, for they walked along so soberly, not one of them trying to run away. Suddenly I heard a loud shouting. I ran to the door to see what was the matter.

"'What do you suppose I saw? Yes, a large flock of sheep, but they were running hither and yon, and the men were shouting so very loud! What was it I saw in the very middle of the flock, bobbing up and down? Was it one of the sheep? No, it could not be, for it had a shining curly head and wore a plaid dress. It looked so much like my own little boy. Yes, there he was, my precious child, walking with the sheep, not knowing the danger he was in, with a drum thrown over his shoulder, on which he was beating as hard as ever he could.

"'Oh!' I cried to the men, 'bring him back, for he will be killed!' But it was hard work to reach him. I was afraid he would have to go to market and be sold. At last, I had him in my arms.

"'Where were you going?'

"'"Doin' to walk to Hi—o," he said.

"'Going away to leave papa and mamma? Kiss me, now, but never frighten poor mamma so again.'

"'He kissed me, and jumped down to play with his little cart.'"

"What a comical boy!"

"I guess he wanted to be a little lamb," laughed Mary.

"Now, it is your turn, Mary."

"I will repeat the old poem, 'The Fox and the Hen,' which my dear nurse used to say to me every night, when she put me to bed."

"That will be fine!"

"Well, listen."

THE FOX AND THE HEN.

A white old hen with yellow legs,
Who 'd laid her master many eggs,
Which, from her nest, the boys had taken
To put in cake, or fry with bacon,
Was roosting in an outer hovel,
Where barrel, bird-cage, riddle, shovel,
Tub, piggin, corn-bag, all together
Were put, to keep them from the weather ;
When an old fox stole in, one night,
As the full moon was shining bright,
Hoping — if he his nose might stick in —
That he might carry off a chicken,
Or, from a window-ledge or shelf,
Might jump and reach the old hen herself.
Her roost, however, was so high,
He saw it was in vain to try,
By all his jumping, to get at her;
" So then," says he, " I think I 'll flatter
The old fool's vanity, — for, look,
Have her I must, by hook or crook;
In fact I 've thought so much about her,
I shall *fare very ill* without her."

Thus then spoke Renard,* smooth and sly,
And thus Dame Partlett† made reply.

Renard. "Good evening, madam ; how d' ye do ?"
Partlett. "I 'm ne'er the better, sir, for you."
   R. "Better ! you need not, can not be,
     You 're always well enough for me."

* The Fox.   † The Hen.

P. "Well, if I am, then, as you own,
 Pray, sir, let 'well enough' alone."
R. "Dear madam, if you only knew
 But half the *love* I feel for you —"
P. "But half!—Nay, be it great or small, sir,
 I rather think, I know it *all*, sir."
R. "Indeed!—Well, madam, that has taught me
 To care for you; and that has brought me
 Thus late to call—perhaps it's rude,
 But, ma'am, *I hope I don't intrude.*"
P. "Intrude!—indeed, sir, but you do."
R. "It grieves me to hear that from you;
 I'll therefore say no more at present,
 Than just to hint that, as it's pleasant—
 (In truth, you know not, shut up here,
 How pleasant 'tis abroad, my dear) —
 And I delight to hear you talk,
 I've called to invite you to a walk."
P. "A walk!—The like who ever heard!
 A quadruped to woo a bird!
 I'm sick, and early went to bed,
 And scarcely can hold up my head."
R. "Sick! My dear lady! What can ail?"
 Indeed, you *do look very pale.*
 I'm sure your illness can arise
 But from the want of exercise;
 Too much confinement fades the fair.
 A pleasant walk, in open air,
 With pleasant company, at night,
 When the moon shines, will set all right.
 And should you tire, I'll call a hack,
 Or, better, take you on my back.

I 'm sure, though I don't mean to flatter,
That one of us would be the fatter
For such a walk ;—nay, never fear
The jealousy of chanticleer.
He shall not harm a single feather
Of your fair neck, when *we're* together.
Your neck !—ay, now I think upon it,
With your white shawl and scarlet bonnet,
You 'll be, by all, both far and near,
Mistaken for a cherub,—dear!—"
P.   "Well, Mr. Renard,—have you done?
If so, I think you 'd better run;
My master 's coming to the hovel.—
You see that broomstick? and that shovel?
You see the door that you came in at ?—
If you 're not off in half a minute,
Instead of fowls, or e'en a chicken,
You 'll get, as you deserve, a kicking."

The wily flatterer dropped his chin,
And out he sneaked, as he sneaked in.

Moral.   The *cunning* seldom gain their ends:
The *wise* are never without friends.

"Who knows a fairy story?"

"I know about Cinderella," replied Kitty.

Just at this moment a loud ringing at the door-bell was heard, and in burst Hugh.

"Hurrah, boys! here comes Charlie Williams, and I 've brought Etta home with me!"

"Did your aunt scold you very much?"

"Yes, she did, but Hugh teased so hard that she let me come this time, but said she would not allow it again, if I disobeyed her rule."

"I think she was just right, my dear," said Aunt Fannie, who had come into the room. "Children must always remember to obey those who have charge of them and are so much older and wiser."

"Well, I do try to remember, but somehow it goes right out of my head."

"I am glad you could come back, for we are going to have a jolly time," said Mary. "We have been telling lovely stories, sitting here in the dark; you ought to have heard them."

"This is 'blind man's holiday,' but let us have some light on the subject," said Hugh.

The tea-bell rang out its invitation, and the children were soon seated around the pleasant tea-table. When they were silent grandpa asked a blessing of the good Father in Heaven upon all the little ones. In after years they often thought how saintly the dear old man looked, as he uttered the simple words. When they had finished, Frances and Mary took him by the hand and led him into the parlor, to the piano.

"Now, grandpa, you must play us your tune, while we play 'London bridge.'"

So the good old man played the tune, over and over again, until the children were tired of singing it.

"Now for 'bear,'" called Hugh, as he ran up stairs, followed by all the company.

Then such a noise as was heard for an hour! It seemed as if a whole den of wild animals had come into the house. They all took turns, one at a time, in being "bear." The others formed into a line, and at a given signal, would run round and round the rooms, until the leader said "Stop!" If any one was so unlucky as to break the line, then the "bear" could catch the stray lamb and carry it off to its den.

At intervals could be heard a voice crying, "Run, now run! If you have any sense left in you, run!" This command was always obeyed, until they sank breathless on the stairs, which was a place of safety.

Although grandpa was quite deaf, he could plainly hear the shouting, and would come to the stairs, saying:

"Children, I am afraid you are making too much noise!"

"Oh! no, sir, *we are very quiet!*"

Nine o'clock came all too soon. They must prepare to go home, wishing "they could stay just a little while longer."

"Why, Frances, my dear child, have you come!" exclaimed Mrs. Grey, as the little girl appeared at the door with Charley, the coachman, whom Mary had sent home with the children.

"Yes, mamma, and such a lovely time as we have had!"

"I think my little girl does have a nice time with her friends, but I am afraid you are very noisy when together, and must trouble Mary's family."

"Oh! no, we do n't. Aunt Fannie and grandpa seem to like to have us come, and never look put out one bit."

"They must be very indulgent, then, to welcome such a group of chattering boys and girls, for such a long visit."

"Mamma, I wish you could think of something beautiful to give Mary for a Christmas present. I have looked at so many things, but do n't know what to buy."

"A nice book is a very useful and pretty present. We will go to a book-store and see if we can find one by the name of 'Truth is

Always the Best.'   It is a charming story, but rather sad."

" Do tell me about it," said Frances.

"Amy, the little heroine, does a wrong act, and in trying to conceal it is obliged to tell many untruths, which do no good, for at last her disobedience is found out. Her sorrow is sincere, and ever after she tries to do just right."

" I should like so much to get that book for her, it must be splendid !"

"We will look about to-morrow, if the day is pleasant. You must not let all these good times take your mind from school, but study faithfully, and then your play-time will be all the more pleasant."

"Yes, mamma, I am trying for one of the diplomas, which the *four* scholars, who get the highest marks in *every thing*, are to have at the end of the year."

" I hope, my dear, you will succeed, but do n't be too much disappointed, if by any chance you are not one of the fortunate."

All this conversation had taken place while Mrs. Grey had been getting Frances ready to go to rest. It was one of the happy events in the day, "this talk with mamma," and Frances was such a chatterbox, she often talked herself to sleep.

This evening she was so tired that after her prayer, " Our Father," had been said, she closed her eyes and was soon in Dream-land.

III

THE SURPRISE

THESE young friends all attended Sunday school, devoting the hours to the study of the Good Word. They dearly loved to learn of the gentle Saviour, who came on earth to teach people how to live rightly, and so loved little children that he said, "Suffer little children, and forbid them not, to come unto me; for of such is the kingdom of heaven."

Frances went with her papa to his church and Sunday school, the other girls attending elsewhere. He had a large society, composed of what would be called the working class, and they looked upon him as a friend as well as a pastor. He visited daily in their homes, and all came to him with their joys and sorrows, always meeting with a kind response. They loved their good minister, and little Frances was a great pet among them.

The Sunday school was a flourishing one, as

the bright looks, the spirited singing, and the good attendance of the children testified.

On the Sunday before Christmas, Mrs. Robbins, the teacher in whose class Frances was, told them again the story of Jesus Christ, of his coming to earth as a little babe, of his gentle life and sad death, of the blessed religion he taught to men, leading them away from evil doing.

" I think, mamma, that I know much better than ever before about Christmas. It is Christ's day, my teacher said; we all must be so happy, and sing praises to his name."

"Yes, my dear, it is a day which brought joy to the world, gave us our beautiful homes and all the blessings of a Christian land."

A busy time it was during Christmas week, and the children made many calls to the stores where the lovely gifts were displayed. Frances remembered all her little friends by some token of love, and bought the book, " Truth is Always the Best," for Mary.

The day before Christmas came, and often during its hours mysterious packages found the way into Mrs. Grey's hands, who carefully placed them out of sight.

There was to be a Christmas-tree at the

church where Mr. Grey preached. Frances was all excitement, and could hardly wait for evening to come. At last the hour arrived which was to bring so much pleasure to the happy company.

The Sunday-school room was tastefully trimmed with evergreen, and in one corner stood a lovely Christmas-tree, its boughs laden with bags of candy, and lit by colored candles.

The children of the school, had prepared a number of recitations, songs and readings, all appropriate for Christmas or Christ's day. The sweet story of his life was told in song and verse, the joyous voices rang out in "Glory to God in the Highest, Peace on Earth, Good will to Men."

Then Santa Claus appeared, to give the sweets to the children, who showed their delight by crowding about the old man and stretching out their hands for the well-filled bags. The absent ones were remembered by the teachers, who sent these tokens of love to their homes.

" What a splendid Christmas eve we have had! I do hope to-morrow will be just as pleasant. I will hang my stocking near the fire-

place, and then Santa Claus can fill it easily."
So chattered Frances on her way to rest.

Christmas Day dawned bright and clear; the
ground was covered with a new fall of snow,
and the boughs of the trees were laden with
the pure white mantle.

When Frances opened her eyes, she had
almost forgotten what day it was, but as soon
as she looked at her stocking, which now was
full not of emptiness but of something real, she
shouted out as loud as she could, "Merry
Christmas!" then as quickly as possible,
jumped up and ran to see what Santa Claus
had brought her.

A number of bundles were on the floor near
the stocking. These she soon opened, and to
her great delight, a *pair of skates* appeared;
then a fine lady-doll, and a bedstead with real
pillows, a lovely book of pretty poems, a blank
book, and a little rocking-chair, just right for
her. The stocking held a box of pencils to
use in school, a package of candy, and a nice
handkerchief, but away down in the toe there
was a small box, which on opening it disclosed
a silver thimble marked, "M. E. S. to F. S. G."

"Oh! mamma, what do you think? Mary has
given me a beautiful thimble; wasn't she a dar-

ling?   Those skates are just what I wanted, and I am going to learn how to skate this very day, if Ed. will only come with me to the Frog Pond."

"Well, my dear, I think we will have breakfast first, for I guess the boys will have to sweep the snow off the pond before any one can skate." When Ed. appeared to hunt up his presents, she danced around him, swinging the skates in the air, crying, "Papa said, 'Christmas was coming,' and so it has, and here are my skates!"

"I guess you won't like them so much, when you have tumbled down a few times."

"I don't believe I shall fall down *very often*, it looks so easy when you see the others going along."

"Well, you try it, that's all I have to say," replied Ed.

"I don't think you ought to discourage Frances, but help her all you can to learn how to use them," said papa.

"Well, I will, but she thinks it is so easy."

"We all have to try and try again before we succeed, and I know my little girl has the right spirit, and can conquer any thing she undertakes."

Just then Mary and Hugh burst in, their cheeks as red as roses.

"Merry Christmas!" resounded on all sides, and such a babel of tongues for a few moments!

"Come along, girls, and have a coast on my new sled; I have it right here at the door."

They were soon on their way to the Common, and such fun as it was for all to go down together over the steep hill!

"I think the thimble was such a nice present, and I thank you very much, Mary," said Frances.

"Well, I think my book is just splendid, and I shall always keep it to remember you by."

"So shall I the thimble, and I am going to learn how to sew right off; then I can mend my own clothes."

"You will be a fine sewer, now you have a thimble. I thought the book, 'Truth is Always the Best,' a very nice choice for you to make. It is always better not to do wrong, but when we do, to be frank and honest about it, and then it will be so much easier to overcome temptation," said Aunt Fannie.

This conversation had taken place in Mary's house, whither they had gone to warm themselves. The little friends had again a pleasant evening, playing games, singing, and telling stories. Happy childhood, that knows no care; truly their lines were cast in pleasant places.

Mr. Grey's work brought him in contact with those who had been denied a great share of this world's blessings, and Frances early learned to sympathize and be tender to those who were thus unfortunate.

Now at this season, when the strains of "Peace on Earth, Good Will to Men," were resounding through the air, it seemed as if all were one family, with one interest, to praise God for all his mercies. So these young friends caught the spirit, and their hearts were filled by the good lessons taught them of love and charity.

After the pleasant holidays, school and lessons were in order. The arithmetic lessons were still very hard for Frances, but by diligent study, she conquered multiplication and waded through division, at last reaching fractions.

Poor child! it was a sore trial, but she took great comfort in her other studies, excelling in all.

The girls were working for the diplomas, and meant always to be found in their places in season. To Mary, that was the very hardest thing to do, but when she took Aunt Fannie's advice of "early to bed and early to rise," she always found it easier to be there before the clock struck nine.

The chief amusement after school now was skating. The ·Frog Pond and also the little lake on the Public Garden were nicely kept for the use of the skaters. A merry scene, to see the little figures glide over the ice "so easily," as Frances said.

Brother Ed. was as good as his word, and helped her a great deal in learning this slippery art. At first she could not let go his hand, in fact had to cling with both hands to his arm. But gaining confidence, she finally conquered, much to her delight. She felt very proud of this attainment, and wanted her papa and mamma to come and see her skate They gratified her wish, thinking she did very nicely, even if she tumbled down a number of times.

"I told her it would n't be so *very easy*," said Ed.

"The more credit then to overcome a difficult task. In your future life, my boy, you will find that the harder we have to work to obtain a certain object, the more we enjoy it when success is ours."

In after years, Ed. thought of his father's words, and the memory of them helped him in his life work.

One Wednesday afternoon Mary came in to see Frances. After they had played awhile, she asked if Frances could come to her house and stay to tea. Mrs. Grey consented, saying "that she must come home *early*."

"I will send her home at eight o'clock *precisely*," said Mary, laughing, as they skipped away.

At dinner that day mamma had said suddenly, "Where can they put their things?"

"Who?" answered Frances, looking with wonder at her.

Mrs. Grey hesitated, but said, "I rather think Carrie Brown may spend the evening with us."

Tea over at Mary's, the girls were playing quietly with their paper-doll books. As Frances happened to be the only visitor, the other noisy games were out of the question. However, they always enjoyed these paper-doll houses. It was something rather new with them, so they were very anxious to finish the rooms as quickly as possible.

This was the plan: each had a blank book of smooth white paper, and then they collected all the pretty pictures, of furniture, chairs, tables, pianos, desks, dishes, silver-ware, vases, stoves, beds,—in fact every thing that was to be found in a real house. These homes were very large and elegant, having beautiful gardens and conservatories; the walls of the rooms being decorated by fine paintings, and the windows draped with costly hangings. Every thing rich and rare was used in the furnishings.

As they progressed, rooms without number were planned, and the houses were not complete without libraries, parlors, banquet-, reception-, and music-rooms, china-closets, nurseries, and art-galleries. They were really lovely and needed much taste to arrange them in a home-like, natural way.

Then, the families that lived in these mansions were all very beautiful, the ladies being noted for their lovely dresses, and the gentlemen for their elegant bearing.

Frances had received her blank book as a Christmas present from Nellie, the girl who helped Mrs. Grey with her house-work. She had known the want of this article which Frances had felt, and kindly remembered her. So she was eager to have her paper-doll book "the very prettiest of all."

Aunt Clara had helped arrange it, although Frances did a great deal herself. "But Auntie could fix the curtains so nicely, and knew just what colors went pretty together," she said.

They had been playing with their books for some time, when Brother Ed. came in, saying, "Come, Frances, hurry up; your mother wants you to come home, for Carrie Brown and Lizzie Peck have come to spend the evening."

He laughed as he spoke, and Mary echoed the laugh. Frances looked curiously at them for a moment, then began to put on her things to go home.

"Good-night, come again," called Mary as they disappeared from view. As they approached the house Frances noticed that it was all ablaze with light, and she could see that the parlor seemed to be full of people, for the curtains had not been drawn down.

"Why, Ed., who are those people in our house?"

"You wait a minute, and you will find out."

Just as he spoke the door was opened by Mrs. Grey, and before Frances could hardly think, she was clasped by Mary, who, followed by Hugh, had arrived at the same time.

As Frances went in mamma said, "My darling, here are some of your friends come to see you this evening."

In a moment, Frances was the center of attraction, and all the company were enjoying the pleasure of seeing her "surprised." After a while she began to realize that this was a real "surprise party."

At first she did not like it, but as her shyness wore off she entered into the spirit of the occasion, joining in the lively games with great glee. As this was a "donation-party," the company were expected to enjoy the "treat" which they had provided. This was a very important part of the fun, and the cake, oranges, and candy rapidly disappeared.

Frances was again very much surprised to have one of the older boys, Georgie Green, present her a pretty gold ring, in the form of two hearts joined together, as a token of love from all the company.

Poor Frances was almost in tears from very diffidence, at this part of the programme, and was so much overcome by her feelings she could n't speak one word, even to thank her kind friends.

At last the party was over, and the house was quiet once more, although the echo of the happy voices came floating back as the young people went homeward.

Ed. broke out suddenly saying, "I think you were awful silly to cry when they gave you the ring. I wish some one would give me a party and bring a gun for a present, so when I go up to Aunt Mira's, next summer, I could shoot woodchucks."

"Well, I could n't help it, for I did n't expect any party at all, and every one kept looking at me when Georgie gave me the ring."

"That was n't any thing to cry for, sis."

"Now, Ed., I think my little girl did nicely, for it was very trying to be so entirely surprised. A big boy like you, of course, never would be overcome, but I hope that you will not have a gun given to you. Now to bed, for to-morrow morning will come very soon."

"I do n't think I really like surprise-parties; but I do think they were so kind to give me such a pretty present," said Frances.

"Yes, I think you are a fortunate little girl to have so many kind friends, and you must always try to live a good and useful life, so that every one may love and respect you."

These little friends had now been to school for nearly six months of the school year, and studied hard, trying to improve from day to day.

Miss French was very fond of "her girls." She often told the master, "that they were the smartest set of scholars she ever saw together, and that they all deserved great credit for the improvement they had made." She knew that they dearly loved to play, but they also were faithful to their school studies.

As Washington's birthday was near at hand, the twenty-second of February, and as it was to be a holiday, the day before had been appointed, to observe it in the schools. The scholars, who had been much interested in the history lessons, had been learning about their own country, and of George Washington, the American general, who was called " The Father of his Country," in honor of his great achievement in bringing to a successful end the Revolutionary war.

The girls had been practising songs and reading selections, which were appropriate to the day. They were to go into the large hall, and certain ones were to take part in the exercises,—some to read, the master to give a short sketch of the life and career of Washington, and all to sing patriotic songs.

The two best readers from each class had been selected, and the choice had fallen on Etta Kendall and Frances Grey.

Frances was very much pleased at the honor, as she had begun to feel quite a "dunce," for the examples had so troubled her that at times she felt really discouraged. Her teacher often said, "It seemed strange that arithmetic should be so difficult for her, as she was quick and apt at every other study."

The day came, and the hall was full of visitors, friends of the scholars, who had been invited to listen to the programme.

The first musical selection was "America," and the hearts of the audience warmed with love for their own beautiful land, as the words,

> "My country, 't is of thee,
> Sweet land of liberty,
> Of thee I sing,"

were repeated by the fresh young voices. Then the master gave an interesting account of the career of the noble man in whose honor the day was kept; of his early life, and of the events which placed him in the position he held, as the leading general of the American army; and finally as the first president of the United

States. After a number of appropriate reading, "Hail, Columbia," was sung with spirit.

Frances had felt very brave before the time had come for her to read, but as the master announced her name she began to tremble, and her heart beat so quickly that she "could hear it thump," as she afterwards said. She gathered up her courage, however, and gave the name of her selection: "Paul Revere's Ride."

After the first few words she felt quite calm, and read the story of this midnight-ride, giving the words with spirit and right emphasis.

PAUL REVERE'S RIDE.

Listen, my children, and you shall hear
Of the midnight-ride of Paul Revere.
On the eighteenth of April, in 'seventy-five,—
Hardly a man is now alive
Who remembers that famous day and year,—
He said to his friend, "If the British march
By land or sea from the town to-night,
Hang a lantern aloft in the belfry-arch
Of the North Church tower, as a signal-light,—
One, if by land, and two, if by sea,
And I on the opposite shore will be,
Ready to ride and spread the alarm
Through every Middlesex village and farm,
For the country-folk to be up and to arm."

.   .   .   .

So through the night rode Paul Revere;
And so through the night went his cry of alarm
To every Middlesex village and farm, —
A cry of defiance, and not of fear,
A voice in the darkness, a knock at the door,
And a word that shall echo forevermore;
For, borne on the night-wind of the past,
Through all our history, to the last,
In the hour of darkness and peril and need,
The people will waken and listen, to hear
The hurrying hoof-beats of that steed,
And the midnight-message of Paul Revere.

—Longfellow.

Her effort was well received, and it was a real triumph for this young girl.

Etta Kendall's selection was "The Landing of the Pilgrim Fathers."

"Stand, the Ground's Your Own, My Braves!" by John Pierpont, was finely read by one of the older girls.

Every one said that the readers did great credit to their teachers, also to the classes to which they belonged. "The Star-spangled Banner," with its spirited words, closed the programme.

That night papa said to Frances, "I am very proud of my daughter, for I know she has made good use of her time, and studied hard to im-

PAUL REVERE'S RIDE.

prove, and I feel sure she will do good in the world and grow to be a useful woman."

"I will try, dear papa, to do as you say, but sometimes it is very hard to be good."

"Yes, my dear, but we must never weary in well doing, and our lives will be all the happier if we always try to do our duty."

The impression made on her mind by the words was never forgotten, and if she was tempted to do wrong, or to shirk a duty, the thought would come to her of the lesson her father taught her that time.

When Annie Bell opened her eyes the next morning, she heard a great noise, the booming of cannon and the ringing of bells. She listened a moment, and then covered her head over with the bed-clothes, for she was really frightened. After a little while she gained courage to peep out again, but still the bells kept ringing.

After a few moments she jumped up and ran into her mother's room.

"Oh! mamma, I am so afraid! There is a terrible fire somewhere!"

"You dear child, it is Washington's birthday, and the bells will ring three times to-day,— morning, noon, and night."

"Oh! so it is, but I didn't remember. We

will have a lovely time, for the girls and boys are going to Music Hall, and we can stay all day."

Before Annie was hardly ready Etta arrived.

"I am going to wear my new plaid dress; isn't it pretty?" said Annie.

"Yes, and auntie finished my brown one, which I like ever so much."

"You will be too early, girls," said Mrs. Bell, "if you go now."

"Oh, no! it opens at ten o'clock, and we want to get there, to march with all the others. Good-bye, dear mamma. I wish you could go with us."

"I should like to go very much, my dear; now have a good time and remember to be a little lady."

Mrs. Bell sighed as the gay young spirits flitted away. She thought of the great affliction which had deprived her of her own health and saddened the life of little Annie. She was always glad to have her enjoy a pleasant time, even if she herself was shut out from any active enjoyment. Annie was a loving child, always considerate of her dear mother, doing little acts of kindness to lighten the weary life, which as an invalid she was forced to bear.

The children ran as quickly as possible to Mary's house.

"Come upstairs, girls; Frances is here, and I am not quite ready.   Where is Kitty?"

"Oh! she's coming sometime!"

Aunt Fannie was curling Mary's hair, which soon lay in shining ringlets about her head.

"Oh! what a lovely dress!" cried the girls, as a new stone-colored cashmere, trimmed with blue, was taken out of the closet.

"Yes, papa let me choose it myself, and I like it ever so much."

She looked very pretty; also little Frances was like a "blue-bell" in her blue dress.

Kitty soon put in an appearance, wearing a garnet dress with blue ribbons, "just the match for her eyes," said Etta.

A happy company, all ready to celebrate the day in good earnest.   Their childhood indeed was full of pleasure, and the path was made smooth by loving friends.   They were hardly old enough to realize their blessings, but unconsciously good thoughts and motives were growing to be a very part of themselves; the sunshine was always about them, and very few clouds came across their sky.

"Girls, are you ready?"

"Not quite, but wait for us."

"We boys are going along first, and we'll see you there."

"They never will go with us girls, Hugh says it looks spoony," said Mary.

"My Brother Ed. always wants to go alone, but mamma says that boys learn to be gentlemen, if they are polite and kind to their sisters. She says that one of her brothers always would walk on the opposite side of the street, when they were going to Sunday school, as he didn't want to be seen with *girls.*

"I guess they will be glad enough to march and drill with us, even if they don't want to go when we do," said Etta

At last Mary was ready, and they skipped over the hill to Winter street, where Music Hall stands.   This hall is very dear to the hearts of Boston people, and has been the scene of many brilliant and happy occasions.   But never a happier company assembled than these bright-eyed, laughing girls and boys, who now were to enjoy the pleasures prepared for them.

The hall was a large one, with two balconies, which were gaily trimmed with flags and bunting; the platform was covered with large pot-plants, so that the musicians were almost screened by them. A full-length picture of Washington, at the end of the hall, was also decorated with flags. Their parents and friends watched them from the balconies.

As the girls entered the hall the orchestra was playing a march, and the persons in charge were busily engaged in getting the young people into order.

"I hope Charlie Howard is here," said Annie, "for I know he will march with me."

"Oh! the boys are all too afraid," replied Kitty.

So it proved, for only a few of them were to be seen, and the girls at last formed into line. Charlie Howard *was there*, but much to the disappointment of Annie, asked Etta to march with him.

Annie felt a very funny sensation, a little twinge of envy, away down deep in her heart, and she almost made up her mind not to march; but Kitty took hold of her arm saying, "Come along, Annie, he will march with you, I know, so don't feel so bad !"

Annie wouldn't have cared, "if she had not said any thing about it."

At last all was ready; the long line of children, mostly girls, each carrying a small flag of red, white, and blue, were soon keeping time with the music. When they were fairly started, the *missing* boys appeared in view, to watch the pretty sight. They had disappeared just at the time they were in demand.

As the girls afterwards said, "How afraid they were to march with us!"

Charlie Howard, however, looked very brave and held his head up high, knowing he had done a gentlemanly act, and that his partner was a very nice little girl.

"That's right," said a gentleman as they marched by. "I like to see a boy polite to his girl friends."

After the march a girl and boy came forward, dressed in Scotch costume, and went through a Highland dance. They looked just like bright birds, skipping around in their fancy plaid dresses and jaunty caps, and every one was delighted with their graceful movements.

Then the girls and some of the boys, — for they had summoned up courage to take a share in the fun, — formed into line for an old-fashioned New England game: " Pop goes the weasel."

It was such fun when the time came to "pop" their heads under the extended arms, and a ripple of merriment could be heard all over the hall.

"Oh! I am so tired! I must rest now," said Mary.

"So am I, but Charlie Howard has asked me to be his partner for the next time, so I think I will," said Annie with a beaming smile.

"There's my Brother Ed. looking in at the door. I hope he has n't come for me to go home yet," said Frances.

Her fears were groundless, as he had only come to view the scene and to tell her "to come home early, for she would get too tired, her mamma had said."

"Let's all go up into the balcony and rest for a while," said Kitty.

They followed her advice, and much enjoyed looking down upon the graceful marchers, stepping so lightly to the lively music. At intervals the orchestra would play a fine selection.

Alas! the time came all too soon for the merry company to depart. As the girls approached Mary's home, a group of boys were seen standing on the steps.

"Oh! there are Charlie Howard and Hugh and Frank Bliss," said Annie with a little laugh.

"Who cares where they are? They always run off and leave us when we go anywhere," replied Kitty.

"When Hugh is alone he is quite polite; but I suppose the other boys plague him if he is seen with the girls," said Mary.

"Halloa, girls! did you have a good time?"

"Splendid!" "Gorgeous!" "Fine!" was echoed on all sides.

"I should think, Hugh, you might have marched with us a little more to-day. Charlie Howard was very polite," said Mary.

"I don't like to march in such a big place. If *you* will have a party I will march every time. All come in and see how nice I have fixed the play-room," said Hugh.

They ran up three flights of stairs, and entered a large room, with a small one adjoining it. It was a very pleasant, sunny place, and the children spent many happy hours at play in this "Museum," as Mary called it. A host of playthings were in sight,—dolls, books, kites, rocking-horses, wagons, doll-houses, were scattered in confusion over tables and chairs.

In one corner was a large basket, in which Tabby, the cat, with her numerous family, was cosily resting, and lying on a soft mat was a beautiful little greyhound, which jumped up with a welcome bark as the children burst into the room.

The boys had trimmed the smaller room with flags, hung a curtain before the door, with a string arranged by which to pull it back, when the performance they had planned should begin.

"Now, boys and girls, I am going to make a speech. We want to have some tableaux and charades, and charge pins for coming in. You must all come here every day to practise, then we will have the show some Saturday afternoon. Won't that be fun! Perhaps we might charge the folks a cent, after a while, when they know it is fine; save up the money and buy something jolly!"

"That will be splendid!"

"We can have 'Babes in the Wood.'"

"Yes, and 'Cinderella,' and the 'Siamese Twins,'" joined in a chorus of voices.

"I think it is jolly to have Washington's birthday; let's give three cheers for George Washington. Now, one, hurrah! Two, hurrah! Three, hurrah!" shouted Hugh.

At this moment Aunt Fannie came running to see what was the trouble; the cook and

Norah rushed up from the kitchen, thinking the house was on fire.

"Oh! it's only Master Hugh, he 'll scare the life out of a body shure!" said Bridget, the cook.

A very tired little girl was Frances, as she crept into her mother's arms to tell her all about the delightful day, and so worn out by the excitement that she fell asleep when she was only halfway through her story.

"Poor pet, I am afraid she is overdoing; but children never realize they are tired until they fairly drop. I think I must say 'no,' once in a while, to all these good times," said Mrs. Grey to her husband.

"Well, my dear, I see so many poor little children in my daily visits, who although deprived of many comforts, are still happy playing together, that I think childhood knows no care in any station of life. As my children grow older I wish them to realize the blessings and privileges given to them, that they in their turn may lend a helping hand, to lighten the burdens of others less fortunate."

"Dear papa," his children and many others did rise up and call him "blessed."

IV

THE SEWING–CIRCLE.

PAPA, may I go with you visiting this afternoon?" said Frances, as she finished her breakfast and prepared for school.

"Yes, my dear, I should be happy to have you go with me, and I know all the children will be very glad to see you. I shall visit families where you have never been, and you can see how some other children live."

As Frances looked around the pretty breakfast-room, with the morning sun shining in, making all look so cheerful, she did think that her home was very nice, and that she ought to be a good child, with so many comforts about her. After dinner mamma dressed her warmly for the walk. Taking hold of papa's hand, she skipped along as happy as could be.

Down the hill they went past stores of all kinds, houses and churches, to the busy street below; then, after walking through a short cut, they entered a narrow alley-way.

In former times this place had been a desirable residence, but now it wore a dilapidated appearance, and seemed as if it was shut out from the world, and that even the sun could not find its way to this out-of-the-way corner. The space in front of the houses was filled by children of all sizes and ages, playing, laughing, and shouting together, seemingly as happy as if they were surrounded by every thing beautiful instead of dreary brick walls.

As Mr. Grey and Frances entered the court a number of the children ran up to them, saying, " Here's the minister and his little girl."

"My mother has gone out washing"; "My sister is home minding the baby"; "May I come to your singing school?" chattered the children

A boy, somewhat larger than the others, who had been sitting on the steps of one of the houses, rose and made way for Mr. Grey and Frances.

"Walk in, sir; mother is out, but will be home soon."

They entered a bare-looking hall and opened the door of one of the rooms on the lower floor. It was not a pleasant place, although quite neat; the bare floor had been washed, the stove blacked, and some pretty plants stood in the windows, in one of which was a canary-bird hopping about in its cage. Two children were playing in one corner of the room. On seeing the visitors, they jumped up, seeming very much pleased. They knew the kind minister and his little daughter.

The little boy was a hunch-back, and his sister was very lame. Poor souls; a hard lot was theirs, but still they seemed happy.

"Well, Lizzie, what have you here?" said Mr. Grey, looking at a curious arrangement in the corner.

"Oh! that's Moses in the bulrushes. My teacher told us about little Moses, and gave us this picture, so we thought we would have him to play with," said Sammy.

Mr. Grey laughed. They had taken an old basket, put in a quilt, on which reposed a doll for Moses, then covered it over with boughs of an evergreen tree which had been thrown away in some ash barrel—probably a part of a Christmas tree.

"Then you like to hear about little Moses, and how the kind princess cared for him, so that he grew up to be a good and useful man."

"Oh! yes, sir," they cried.

Just then the mother of the family, a slender-looking woman, came in. She was a widow and worked hard to keep a home for her little ones. She looked upon Mr. Grey as a friend, and came to him with her burdens. He helped her to bear them, and sent many comforts to this little home.

"I am indeed glad to see you, sir, and I wish to thank you for getting my boy Jim such a good place. He can help us now, and maybe I can get along easier-like," she said.

"I hope he will prove to be a good, faithful boy, and that his employer may have reason to place confidence in him.   Remember," said Mr. Grey, laying his hand on the head of the older boy, "that *honesty* is the foundation-stone upon which success in life is gained. Keep strictly to that, and every one will respect you."

"I want to go to work, sir, but mother says I ought to have more schooling."

"Yes, I wish he could get a good start in his books, and then he might learn something that would pay him well, sir."

"That is true; a good education is of great value to any one; something that can never be taken away. If you can keep him in school as you wish for a while, he could obtain some desirable position."

" He 's very smart, sir, at learning, and I hate to put him to drudgery just yet."

" He must make good use of his time now, so that when it is necessary, he can use the knowledge gained. Come, Frances, we must go, as I have a number of calls to make this afternoon." So saying good-bye to the family, they left little Moses still asleep in the bulrushes.

" Where are you going now, papa ? "

" I think we will call on Auntie Clark."

" What, that little bit of a woman ? "

" Yes, she is small."

They walked through one or two streets, entered a busy thoroughfare, which had the royal name of Prince, but at this time, the princely look was gone, as the houses which had been comfortable were now in a poor condition. In each house numerous families were living, in what had formerly served for *one* family only. The doorways were crowded with children, and the streets with teams of all descriptions. A number of stores displayed the necessaries of life; in one window strings of sausages kept company with a lean-looking goose. Next door, some second-hand clothing, in the shape of coats and dresses, was swinging in the breeze. A pawn-shop sign was displayed; relics of better days were seen in the shape of watches, rings, and articles of every kind.

Frances kept tight hold of her papa's hand, for she did n't really like this place. He opened the door of one of the houses, into a small, dark hall, from which led directly a pair of stairs; then up two more steep flights; at last they stopped, and Mr. Grey's knock was answered by a little old lady, whose beaming smile showed her delight in seeing these visitors.

" Come in, sir! I 'm glad indeed to see you; this is your little girl? Dearie, come and kiss auntie, she 's proud to welcome you to her home. I was hoping you would call, sir, for I have been sick, and that accounts for my not being at church last Sunday. It 's the new-ragedy, sir, takes me all of a sudden; but I got the groceries and coal; many thanks to you, sir; you never forget old auntie."

She talked on so fast, that Mr. Grey could only bow his head in answer.

" Sit right down here, sir, in the big chair. *That* belonged to my husband, who 's dead and gone, sir, and many an hour's comfort he's taken, sitting in that very chair. That was when we were comfortable-like, with a little bit laid by for a rainy day, but it all went, and now poor auntie is left alone."

She wiped her eyes as she spoke, but in a moment the sunny smile came back.

"Now, dearie, do n't you want to see my cat and her kittens? Come over to the corner, and I will show them to you."

Frances soon had the pleasure of seeing big black Dinah and her five little ones, cuddled warmly in a wooden box filled with straw, which auntie had fixed for them.

As she looked about the room she thought it was the smallest place, with the most things in it, she had ever seen. It was an attic room, having only one window in it, and contained a bed, stove, table, an old-fashioned bureau, a sea-chest, which had belonged to her husband, who had been a sailor, a number of chairs, some pictures, and a little mantel-piece was loaded with shells of all sizes and curious ornaments, treasured by the old lady as relics of better days. There was no curtain at the window, but it was covered by blooming plants, which seemed to rival each other in a profusion of blossoms. The old lady busied herself in cutting some of the pretty flowers, and gave them to Frances, "to take home to her mother, with love from auntie, hoping she would come to see her soon."

Taking leave of the old lady, they wended their way down the steep stairs.

" I thought, papa, you were going to take me to see some of the children ? "

" So I am, my dear, but I knew Auntie Clark would enjoy seeing my little girl. Although not a child in years, yet she is one in mind, as her whole thought is in the days of her youth, that are past and gone. Now we will walk up Salem street, and you can see the old North Church, or Christ Church, from whose tower Paul Revere saw the lanterns gleaming out, as he waited in darkness on the opposite shore, that eventful night which was the beginning of the struggle for liberty and the formation of the United States. Here it is, and that is the tower, which also contains the musical bells sent over as a present from Queen Anne of England."

Frances looked curiously at the plain, stone building, but could hardly realize the facts, as all looked now so quiet about it. As they passed, the bells rang out an invitation to enter.

"I think there is a vesper service, and we will go in," said Mr. Grey.

As they entered, the dim light in the church seemed to throw shadows over the scene. Frances looked with wonder at the ancient relics about her. It was nearly dark when they came out, but as Mr. Grey wished to see the sexton of his church, they stopped at one of the houses on Salem street.

"Right glad to see you, sir! Come in, don't be afraid if we are crowded; we always make you welcome. The children are eating their supper, for I approve of their going to bed early, then I can have time to work, sir," said a hearty-looking woman, as she dusted a chair with her apron.

"So this is the little girl, come to see all my family together. They make a great deal of work, sir, but I couldn't spare one of them."

The room was very small to begin with; the table around which the children sat was large; there were eight of them just like steps, all girls but one, a black-eyed boy, who, being the youngest, ruled the entire family. He was enjoying a huge slice of bread laden with molasses, and his face corresponded with his supper. So there was not very much room left for visitors.

The children, however, were delighted to see Frances, and jumped down from the table to gather about her, eager to show their treasures in the shape of blocks, dolls, and picture-books, which kind friends had given them. Even little Jack wanted to exhibit his tin-horse and cart. They had all fared well at the Christmas festival, and were very proud to have Frances come to see their playthings.

"This is my new dolly."

"See my pretty new blocks."

"Here is my lovely book, teacher gave me," chimed in the little ones.

"They are all very pretty," said Frances.

Mr. Grey, who had been busily talking, said "Come, my dear child, mamma will be wanting to see us at home. Say good-bye to these little folks, and ask them to come see us some day."

"Thank you kindly, sir, I am fearful you would repent the bargain if they should all come at once," laughed the mother. "I'll let them come by twos, sir, and I guess even then you'd be glad to have them go home; they are great romps."

"You ought to live on a farm, and put them

out in the fields to grow, like the trees and green grass."

"Ah! sir, how I wish we were in our native village, with plenty of air to breathe, instead of living in this close place," and the good woman heaved a sigh, as the picture of her country home rose before her. "But I'm thankful we keep well, sir; it is a great blessing."

"Yes, with good health we can brave almost any trouble and not repine. Now good day, I shall call again soon."

"God bless you, sir; you have indeed been a kind friend to us."

"Tum aden," shouted little Addie.

It was quite dark as they emerged from the house, so they hurried through the neighboring streets, which were now brightly lighted, and were soon at home. Oh! how cosy and warm it looked, as mamma opened the door, and *how good* the hot supper tasted!

"Well, my dear, how did you like visiting?"

"Very much, but I don't think I should like to live there always. We saw *all* the little Wood children, but I don't really think I should like to have quite so many children in *this* family."

Mrs. Grey laughed. "I guess you are afraid

mamma couldn't give you so much attention if she had seven little girls instead of one."

Brother Ed., who was studying his lessons, looked up from his books, saying, "I wish I had some brothers, so we could go hunting and fishing, and have jolly fun; girls are no good to tramp around."

"Well, my dear son, you must remember that girls are not so strong as boys, but are very useful in their own way, and all brothers ought to appreciate their sisters, for they are like sunshine in a house."

"Oh! they are good enough, but they can't play like boys."

"As you grow older and wiser, you will be better able to judge of the merits of the question, and perhaps you may learn that the world owes its progress to the influence of good women who were once little girls."

"I am going to call with papa some other day and mean to visit a primary school, where most of them are poor little ones, taught by a good lady who loves them very much."

"I hope my daughter and son will always be interested in all good work, and do their share in the world to help those who are not so fortunate."

At recess one day Mary eagerly said, " Oh! girls, do n't you want to have a sewing-circle, and make dresses for the poor beggar girls? A very ragged child came to our gate, begging this morning. She was shivering with cold, and I told Aunt Fannie to give her one of my dresses, but she was so small we could n't find one to fit her. So Aunt Fannie said that perhaps I could help make one, but it will take me too long by myself, and so I want you all to help me. Auntie said we could each give ten cents, and buy cotton cloth to make her some warm underclothing, and she would make over a dress and sack of mine to fit her."

" I can't sew very well," said Kitty.

" I can't either, but I shall use my new thimble," said Frances.

" No matter, we can learn to sew, and we will begin next Saturday afternoon," replied Mary.

" I thought you were going to practise for tableaux; Hugh said so," put in Etta.

" So we are, but we must sew first. Etta, you can sew nicely."

" Yes, I can do very well for a little girl, aunt says. I have to help make my own clothes. I am learning to cook, and can make real good one-egg cake."

" Well, now, girls, remember what I have told you, and be sure to have ten cents to-night ready, so we can buy the cotton cloth after school."

Frances burst into the house that noon, crying, " Where's papa?   I want papa!"

" My dear child, what is the hurry? " said his voice from the library.

" Oh! I must have *ten cents* to dress up all the little beggar girls, and Aunt Fannie is going to teach us to sew to-morrow, and we are going to make every thing *lovely* for them, then they will never go ragged again! "   She stopped to take breath.

" Only ten cents?   I am afraid that sum of money would not buy very much."

" But we are to put *all* the money together, I mean, and that will be a good deal to begin with.   Don't you think it will be nice, mamma? "

" When you can tell me more about the plan, I can judge much better."

" But I want the ten cents this noon, so we can buy things after school to-night," said Frances, with a little sob.

" My dear child, you shall have it, but you must not get so excited that you hardly know what you are saying," said papa, handing her a bright new dime.

" I thought you did n't like it."

" You dear child, you know mamma and papa are glad to have their daughter think of the needs of others, and are always willing to help her do so. You must tell us the whole story some other time, for we should like to hear about the plan very much."

" Now I am going to use my lovely silver thimble! Mamma, why do n't you make me mend my own clothes ? "

" I have such very hard work to keep my little girl in the house after school-hours, that I am afraid her clothes would suffer if left to herself. She likes to play with the other children so well that the time for work flies away."

" Etta can sew lovely. Her aunt keeps her in to sew for her, so I do n't think she can come to the Sewing-Circle very much."

" Etta is a very diligent, capable girl, and will find that this plan of teaching her to help herself will be of great use to her in after years, although now it seems hard, when she wants to play with the children. I will begin this week and teach you how to mend stockings nicely."

" Oh ! do n't *this week*, for I must go to the

Sewing-Circle, and I can learn every thing there, and we will have to buy the cloth and perhaps cut out the things."

Mrs. Grey laughed. " I guess you will have your hands full, if that is the case."

That afternoon, as there was no recess, the girls could n't talk over the plan, but nodded their heads to each other and held up the ten-cent pieces as a sign of good luck. Etta even had one, and looked very happy about it, for she had been doubtful if her aunt would allow her to take part in the plan. It was arithmetic afternoon, and the closest attention was needed, to solve and explain the examples, which were in division of fractions.

Poor Frances was quite in despair, as every one of her answers was wrong, and the more she tried to get them right, the more puzzled she became. The teacher explained again and again, but it was of no use; her patience quite gave out, and she burst into tears.

" Do n't give up like that, my dear ! You have only to remember a certain principle, and it will all come right. I think we will rest for a while and have some reading," said Miss French.

Frances recovered her spirits and was able

to read a nice selection, for which Miss French praised her. She felt sorry for the little girl, and knew it was only a want of courage and reliance in herself, which she needed, to conquer this, to her, difficult task.

At last four o'clock came, and the moment school was dismissed the girls rushed over the hill to Mary's house, where they were to consult.

" It's too bad you cried, Frances," said Mary, "but the examples were pretty hard. I did n't get mine all right."

" I think arithmetic is the very worst study in the whole world, and I do n't see any *use* in it," said Frances.

" Well, I suppose there is, or we would n't have it."

" Do n't talk any more about *that ;* it won't do any good," said Etta.

They had asked Julia Shaw to join them, so with twenty cents which Mary gave, Aunt Fannie and grandpa twenty, and Hugh five, all he had left of his weekly allowance, they had almost a dollar, which Hugh said "he would make up, as soon as he could save enough."

" Now, Aunt Fannie, how much cloth shall we buy? I will put it down on paper, so we shall be sure to remember. Six yards cotton cloth," repeated Mary. "What kind?"

"Unbleached,' chimed in Etta ; "it's stronger and easier to sew."

"That's a long word to write, but never mind. Three yards calico for aprons, one card of white porcelain buttons, two spools thread, and needles."

"Oh! we 've got plenty of them."

"Well, I guess that is all, so come now, for the stores will be closed. I 'll take the money and put it in my new pocket-book papa gave me Christmas," said Mary.

They started out in great glee, much delighted with this new mission. Almost before they knew it, they were in one of the large dry-goods stores, and must collect their scattered senses, so as to be able to make the purchases.

"Wait a minute, girls! I declare, I've forgotten what we wanted. Oh! here is the list I wrote, and that will tell me! Now let me see if the money is all right. Yes, and I do hope we have enough money. Whom shall we ask, and where shall we go for cotton cloth? I do n't see any here."

"I do n't believe they keep it," said Kitty.

" Etta, you ask that clerk, who is looking at us, if they do have it."

" I do n't dare to, for I really think he will laugh at us."

" *I* will ask him, I 'm not afraid ! " said Mary. " Please, sir, do you keep cotton cloth ? "

" Plenty of it, miss," said he with a smile. " You go to the right-hand counter near the side door, and you will find all you can buy."

" Thank you, sir ! "

The other girls had stood about Mary, eagerly awaiting his answer, and their faces were beaming with smiles as they turned away in the direction he had pointed out. They looked so happy that it was like sunshine in the dull store, and the tired, gray-haired clerk said to his companion who stood near :

" How happy childhood is !—so free from care and perplexity ! Those children have some plan in their heads, I warrant you, for their eyes sparkled like stars while they listened to me." His thoughts wandered away to his own boyhood, and the green fields, the scent of the new-mown hay, and the little brook where he watched the tiny minnows come and go, the quiet farm-house and the lowing cattle, the tinkling of the bells, lulling him to sleep after the dear mother had heard his evening prayer, all came back to him, as he looked after that happy company.

All unconscious they proceeded to the counter.

" Have you any cotton cloth ? "

" Yes, miss ; what kind would you like ? "

" I 've forgotton ; it 's on the paper ; I can't read it, I wrote it in such a hurry ! "

" Why, it 's *unbleached* cotton we want," spoke up Etta.

" Oh ! yes, that is t—unbleached, sir · and please cut off six yards."

" Fifty cents, miss," said the clerk, as he rolled up the bundle.

Mary counted out the money, saying, " I 'm glad it did n't cost any more, for now we can get all the other things and have a little left."

" Where is the calico ? "

" On the other side, near the stairway."

They trotted across the space and soon were trying to decide which color and pattern to choose.

" Is she a pretty little girl? "

" Well, she did n't look very pretty."

" Never mind, she 's just as good and must have some nice aprons."

"How do you like pink and white, miss?"

"That's lovely, but I am afraid it is too light."

"Do get that, it will make her look pretty; pink is becoming to people with dark hair," said Frances.

"She has bright eyes, but was so dirty I could hardly tell how she did look. Well, you may give me three yards of that pink," said Mary.

She paid thirty cents for it, and now had the buttons and thread to buy, which were soon obtained. The gas had been lighted in the store before their purchases had been made, and now the weary clerks were arranging the goods to leave until the next day's work began.

"Why, girls, it's real dark! We must run, for aunt told *me* to be sure and be home by tea-time."

"Was she willing you should join the Sewing-Circle?"

"Well, I had to tease her hard, and I shall have to sew just as much at home, she says."

"I'm so glad you can help us, for you are a good sewer."

So they talked as they ran along, and after saying good-bye at Mary's door, with the parting words, "Be sure and come Saturday," ringing in their ears, they were soon all safely at home.

Kitty Lee was chattering at the tea-table over the new plan, and "what fun it was to go shopping."

"We were rather afraid to ask at first, for fear the clerks might laugh at us, but they were real kind, and we found just what we wanted."

"It was enough to make any one laugh to see so many girls buying *one* thing," said Jennie, the older sister.

"Well, they didn't laugh, but were very polite."

"If you dress the child up so fine, she can never go begging again," chimed in another member of the family.

"Well, we don't wish her to, but she can go to school if she has some good clothes, and we are going to tell her so, Mary says."

"I think it is a very nice plan, and I like to see children thoughtful of the good of others," said Mrs. Lee.

On Saturday, Frances could hardly wait to eat her dinner, she was so impatient to go to Mary's house and "begin the Sewing-Circle."

"They will all be there before I am, and I

must go, for we want to get ever so much done this afternoon, and we are to practise for the tableaux besides, so I must go, really, mamma!"

"I don't think Mary will be hardly through with her dinner, if you go too early."

At last she was ready to start, with basket in hand, in which reposed the precious thimble, a pair of scissors, and a needle-case. She felt as if she were really going "to do wonders in the art of sewing," mamma said. "The dear child! how she does love to be with her little friends, and I can not have the heart to keep her from them, however much I desire her company."

"Well, my dear wife, a happy childhood gives the color to one's future life, making it seem full of brightness, even if the dark clouds come near sometimes. A sunny disposition is one of the greatest blessings, bringing joy and comfort into any family. Innocent pleasures and interests keep children happy, besides giving them new ideas of helpfulness in this world of ours," said papa.

Although Frances had started early, she found some of the other girls had arrived before her.

Their merry voices were a guide to her, and she quickly ran upstairs to the play-room. A busy scene it was. Aunt Fannie sat by a table, cutting out and preparing the work, which the girls were to finish. Etta and Mary had begun to sew, while Kitty was listening to Aunt Fannie, as she kindly told her the best way to arrange her task. Hugh and Frank Bliss were busy in the little room, "fixing up" for the rehearsal, which seemed to need a great deal of hammering, and they kept up such a racket that the girls were almost out of patience with them.

"Well, I'm glad you have come at last, Frances! We were afraid something had happened so you could n't be here," said Mary.

"I wanted to come an hour earlier, but mamma thought it was too soon and that I should interrupt your dinner."

"Oh, no! we had it early, on purpose to have lots of time to work. What would you like to sew?"

"Something easy; I can hem pretty well."

"Then you can help on this apron, Kitty may take the other one, and we will see which is the best seamstress," said Aunt Fannie.

It was hard, at first, for the little fingers to

make the stitches just right, but perseverance does wonders, and the work looked quite nice. Their tongues flew faster than their fingers, planning how they should do all this work "just as soon as they could, so the poor child might look nice," said Mary.

"Are you going to put on these clean clothes when she is so dirty?"

"Oh, no! we must give her a bath."

"Perhaps she won't like it."

"Well, she must like it, or not have the clothes. I am going to put her right into the bath-tub, the day we dress her up," Mary said decidedly.

The children laughed at the idea, but thought it a good one.

Mary, who had been looking out of the window, exclaimed, "There she is!"

"Whom do you mean?"

"Why, the poor child! I want her to stop a minute, so Aunt Fannie can measure her."

She threw open the window, calling to her to wait, and then ran downstairs, appearing in a few moments with the girl, who looked frightened, held tight by the hand.

"There, Aunt Fannie, *now* you can measure her."

"Come to me, little girl. I should like to try on this dress and sack."

She did as they wished, but seemed very timid, hardly daring to look at the strangers. After Aunt Fannie had finished the fitting, Mary said: "Here, little girl, take this orange and be sure to come again in a day or two, for we shall want you to try on other things."

The child took the orange, but could hardly stop to say "thank you," ran down the stairs and disappeared from sight, basket in hand.

"I do n't think she is very pretty!" "How snarly her hair looked!" "We must buy her a pair of shoes!" were some of the excited remarks made by the children.

"They cost too much."

"Well, we must find a pair somewhere for her."

"I guess *my* boots would fit her, and I have two or three pairs I can give away" finished Mary.

After this they settled themselves to work for a short time.

"Stop your sewing, girls. Now for the tableaux," cried the boys, as they dashed in among them, scattering thimbles, thread, and sewing in all directions.

This proceeding finished the "Circle" for that day, and after the girls had collected their stray belongings, they folded up each article of clothing carefully, and placed them in a box, which Mary said "was the society work-box."

Then began such a din that poor Aunt Fannie fled for quiet to her own room.

"Now, girls, listen to the manager! Let's have Cinderella first. I want Frances to be Cind, for she is so meek-looking (when she wants to be). Kitty and Etta can be the haughty sisters, for they are tall and can scowl at poor little Cinderella. Then Mary must be the Fairy Godmother, and I will crack the whip when the coach comes to take Cinderella to the ball," shouted Hugh. "You must have on an old dress that will come off easy, when I twitch the strings on it, with a pretty one under it, and you will be a lovely princess," added he. "That's Scene One, and then Charlie can be the Prince, come to find his bride in Scene Two, when all you girls try on the lost slipper, which only fits the ragged Cinderella, who again throws off her old clothes, when the Godmother touches her with the wand. I'll have some red powder to burn, and that will make you all look fine. Now take your places for Scene One. Do you understand?"

"Yes! yes!" was echoed on all sides.

"You must keep very still when the curtain goes up, but you can wink, only be careful not to jerk your heads or twist your mouths, for that would spoil the scene."

At last, after much drilling, the young manager was satisfied.

"We are all too large for Babes in the Wood," said one of the girls.

"I will bring my little sister," said Kitty.

"I guess I can get my little brother to be one of the Babes," said Julia.

"That will be nice."

"Frank Bliss can be one of the robbers, and I guess I can get Charlie Howard to be the other one," said Hugh.

"That will be fine! I know he will come," said Annie Bell.

"Oh! of course you would like it, we all know," laughed Kitty.

"Well, he is a nice boy, and *I* shall think it splendid if he will help us, so do n't blush too much, Annie, for we all think just as you do. Aunt Fannie says he is a little gentle-man, for he always tips his cap whenever he meets her. She says that when boys are polite to older people, it is the sign of a kind heart, and that such a boy will make a good man."

"Oh! hear the lecture! Come, Mary," put in Hugh, "mount this chair and give us the rest."

"That's *all* I have to say just now, but I hope *you* will think of it whenever you meet your friends."

"Oh, bother! do n't talk!"

"Now, company, we are to have one or two scenes from The French Spy, and I will tell you about it later," said Hugh.

The children had been so busy that they had not noticed the weather; but now Hugh exclaimed, "Hurrah, boys! See the big flakes of snow coming down so fast!"

"Why, it has been snowing ever so much, for every thing is just covered, and it 's drifting!"

"I guess we are going to have another big storm."

As it was after six o'clock, the children hastily prepared to go home. They plunged into a snow-drift, but the boys went ahead, to make a path for the girls. They all thought it fine fun to walk in single file, and laughed all the way home.

"Good-night!" "Good-bye!" was said, and they separated, after an afternoon of real pleasure and also profit. They had been learning lessons in patience, kindness, and good-will toward all, and their dreams must have been full of happy thoughts.

V.

THE LITTLE STRANGER.

HE storm kept on all night, and in the morning it was still snowing hard. As Frances opened her eyes she saw the great flakes tumbling down, one after the other, as if having a race.

"Oh! how pretty they look, but when do you suppose it will ever stop?"

"We can hardly determine that, my dear, but I do n't believe it will reach the top of the house, as it did when I was a little girl and was staying with my grandma."

"Oh! do tell me about it!"

"I will do so, perhaps, this afternoon, but now we must go downstairs to breakfast."

How comfortable the pleasant room looked, with the inviting table spread for the morning meal, in contrast to the storm and wind blowing so furiously outside!

A safe place for the children home was at such a time as this, and when so many comforts were to be enjoyed, a blessed privilege it was, to all members of the family, to have such a haven.

After breakfast mamma said, as they stood looking out of the window, "I guess March will go out like a lion."

"What do you mean?"

"If the last week or days of the month are stormy we call it like a 'lion roaring,' but if pleasant and mild, like a 'lamb.'"

Mr. Grey was preparing to go to his morning service despite the storm. Ed. appeared, wearing his great coat and rubber boots, to accompany his father.

"Oh! mamma, I want to go with them," exclaimed Frances, as she saw the preparations.

"I am afraid you would get lost in a snow-drift."

"I can put on my rubber boots, and follow on after they have made a path, and I do want to go so much to Sunday-school."

"Do n't talk, sis, you would tumble down, the very first step you took ; girls never can stand up straight," said Ed.

"I think my little girl quite brave, but my big boy is much stronger, of course, and can make his way through where his little sister could not venture."

"I will tell you the story which we spoke of this morning, if you will not trouble me about what is really impossible for you to do," said mamma.

Ed. went out of the door with great zest, but had only taken a step or two, when down he tumbled and disappeared in a snow-bank, but came in sight, looking like a snow-man. Mamma and Frances laughed, to think that his boasted skill had not held him up. He did not look back, but plunged along as fast as he could.

"I think, my dear, we will look over the Sunday-school lesson."

So they read about the gentle Jesus, how lovely he was in his youth, and of his going about preaching to all those who would listen to him, speaking to them in parables or stories, so that they might understand him. The lesson for that day was about the sower, and what happened to the seed which he sowed.

"My teacher told us what the story meant last Sunday, and we were to repeat it to-day."

"You can think that I am the teacher; first read the parable, then tell me what it means," said Mrs. Grey.

Frances read: "Behold, a sower went forth to sow; and when he sowed, some seeds fell by the wayside, and the fowls came and devoured them up. Some fell upon stony places, where they had not much earth; and forthwith they sprung up because they had no depth of earth. And when the sun was up they were scorched; and because they had no root, they withered away. And some fell among thorns, and the thorns sprung up and choked them. But others fell into good ground, and brought forth fruit, some a hundred-fold, some sixty-fold, some thirty-fold."

"Well, my dear, what was the meaning of this little story, which Jesus told to the people who were gathered about him."

"Teacher said that the sower was a farmer, who went out in the spring-time to plant his ground; that our hearts were the fields and gardens. If we let the good seed fall without taking care of it, that it would be lost to us; that if our hearts were hard like a rock, the seeds could not grow, and if our minds were full of impatience, disobedience, and carelessness, that the thorns would kill our good thoughts, if we did n't try very hard to help it. But if we every day did our duty at school and at home, if we were kind to each other and obeyed our parents, then our lives would be useful, we might do much for others less fortunate in the world, and grow to be good men and women."

"I think your teacher has taught you a very true lesson, and if you remember these words they will always serve to help you in life. We must strive to mark each day by some kind act or word, some duty done, and then from day to day the good seed will grow and yield a large harvest."

"I have some new verses to read to you, and I think they are beautiful."

"I should be very much pleased to hear them."

"Now listen:"

> "Shepherd of thy little flock,
>   Lead us to the shadowing rock
>   Where the richest pastures grow,
>   Where the living waters flow.
>
> "By that pure and silent stream,
>   Sheltered from the scorching beam,
>   Shepherd, Saviour, Guardian, Guide,
>   Keep us ever near thy side."

"I have put these verses in my Bible, so I can always know where they are if ever I forget them."

It had stopped snowing, and the sun was shining. Just at this moment papa and Ed. appeared, making valiant struggles to get up the hill, but it was hard work, and when they reached the house, were glad to stop and take breath. Frances ran to open the door, saying, "Was I the only one absent in my class?"

"No, indeed! I think but two were able to be there, and they lived quite near the church," answered papa.

"You ought to be glad you did n't go, for I tumbled myself," said Ed., looking rather confused, as he knew she had seen his first mishap.

After dinner Mr. Grey again went away, saying that he should go to the Sailors' Home and stay to tea, so that he might be near for the evening service. Frances had been diligently reading her library book, which Ed. had kindly brought from Sunday school, and was feeling rather tired, when her heart was gladdened by seeing Mary and Hugh approaching the house.

"How brave you are to come out in this deep snow!" she cried.

"Oh! It 's just lovely, and the men are clearing the sidewalks, so I guess we can go to school to-morrow," answered Mary.

They had talked busily for some time, when the twilight came stealing in upon them.

"Where's mamma? I want her to tell us the story about the snow-storm when she was a little girl."

"Oh! that will be lovely, and now is just the time for story-telling, as it is getting dark."

Mamma came at their bidding, and the girls gathered closely about her. Ed. made believe he did n't care to hear the story, but sat at the window, looking out. Hugh, however, joined the group.

Mamma began: "When I was a little girl, even younger than any of you, I was sent to spend the summer with my grandpa and grandma in New Hampshire, many miles away from my home. I had for a playmate an aunt, who was only a few years older than myself.

"We lived outdoors nearly all the summer, playing in the fields, having a big rock for our house, riding back to the barn on top of the last load of hay, when the horn was blown for supper. We were only indoors at night, when tired out with play we crept into bed.

"So the time passed until cold weather came. Grandma told me that my dear baby sister was sick, and that I must stay a little longer with her. I was very contented, for now a new pleasure came, as the fall school began, and I was to go with the other children.

"After the snow was on the ground, the boys used to draw the girls on sleds up the steep hills, then at night coast down these hills to their homes. It was rare fun, and many happy hours we spent.

"Sometimes we would all stay in the evening and have a spelling match. It was very exciting, for the neighbors would come in to listen to us, and we were very proud to do well. Then the two lines would stand up and try to spell each other down. I was the very smallest child in school, but I always wanted to stand up with the others.

"One evening the scholars had hardly failed in a single word. At last the teacher waited a moment, then looked up with a twinkle in his eye, and gave out the word 'cat-e-chu-men.' They could spell the first part of the word right, *cat-e*, but when it came to the middle *chu*, that would be either *cu* or *que*, which of course was wrong.

"As it came my turn to spell, oh! I longed to get it right and take the head of the line. The word was given to me, but, alas! I also made a mistake. So they all had failed on both sides. That ended the evening's work.

"As we were going home snow-flakes began to fall, and the next morning it was a snow-storm in real earnest. Grandma thought that the girls better stay at home that day. The storm kept on, not only one, but three days. When we were tired of playing with our dolls, and in fact of every thing else, we would stand at the windows and watch the flakes come down.

"The house was on the slope of a hill, and as no other was near, all we could see was fields stretching away, covered with the white snow.

"'Oh! grandma, will it ever stop?'

"'I guess it will before a great while, but it is a regular old-fashioned snow-storm.'

"This was the first day, but by noon of the second the snow had piled up so high that we could not see out of the windows. The boys did not venture to school that day, but were kept busy in taking care of the horses, cows, sheep, and hens, and digging a path from the house to the barn. Aunt Sophy and I would go with them to see that the pets were all right, and although we were there only a short time, the path would be covered up before we could get back to the house. the snow came so fast.

"As grandpa's house was built one story and a half, as they say, with a sloping roof, the snow had drifted so high that it came up above the door, so that we were completely shut in.

"On the morning of the third day, it was still snowing, but about noon it began to lessen, and in an hour or two had nearly ceased. The men and boys, as soon as possible, began to break out paths from the house to the road. This was hard work and took them a long time, for the snow was very deep. They worked until dark, and were up bright and early, the next morning. After breakfast we heard the boys calling us to come to the front door. This is what we saw:

"The snow was so deep and solid that, as the path was cut through, it stood firm and had formed an arch from the door to the road. As we stood looking out, a very sad sight we witnessed. A dear little babe, who lived in the house above us, had died, or rather been taken to its home in Heaven, during this fierce storm, and was now safe from all harm, but its tiny form was to be buried to-day Two large oxen drawing an ox-sled, on which was the small coffin that held the little one, came in view. They went very slowly, as the way was rough, but at last disappeared over the hill. Grandma said that the mother had two very sick children at home, so could not leave them to go with the little one, but the faithful father followed the wee mite to its resting-place."

"It seemed too bad," said Frances.

"Yes, but as grandma said, the dear Jesus would care for it, and the good angels welcome the little spirit to their beautiful home."

"What did you do in the evenings?" asked Mary.

"Well, we would sit down before the big fire-place in the kitchen, where the big logs were burning, and put apples before the fire to roast. The boys would pop corn, and one evening grandma made molasses candy."

"Oh! how jolly! I wish I could have been there when they roasted a pig," broke in Ed., suddenly.

"Are you listening, my son? I thought you did n't care to hear this little story."

"Well. I could n't help hearing," replied Ed., rather ashamed of himself, and drawing his chair up nearer the circle.

"I wish I had been a little girl then, for it

must have been fine to sit down before the big fire-place and see the great sparks fly out," said Frances.

"I think it would have been the best fun to dig through the snow," said Hugh.

"Oh! sliding down the long hills was the jolliest of all," put in Ed.

"Well, I would have liked the summer time, and the riding home on top of the hay," finished Mary.

"Is that all the story?"

"Yes, I think so for this time, but perhaps I will remember another some other day. I will tell you what we did one Sunday morning, and you will see that we were not always good children."

The young folks had been so interested that they hardly knew how late it was, until the clock struck nine.

"Why, Hugh, we must go home, for auntie will be worried about us," said Mary.

They all thought this a pleasant ending to a stormy day, thus hearing about what happened when mamma was a little girl.

"It is almost time for dear papa to come home, and here we are all in the dark," said Frances.

After Ed. had lit the gas, Mary and Hugh departed.

"It has been such a lovely Sunday at home, but I thought in the morning it would be a dull day staying indoors. I have studied my lesson, read my library book, and this evening mamma has told us a nice story about a big snow-storm, when she was in New Hampshire," said Frances to papa.

"I think, my daughter, the secret of your happiness has been the good spirit with which you gave up your own desire to the wishes of mamma. We are always rewarded by feeling happy when we do right, although we may be disappointed," answered papa.

The next morning the sun was shining, and the sidewalks nicely cleared, so that the children could go to school without any trouble.

Although the snow had fallen to quite a depth, the sun was so high that its warmth soon caused it to rapidly disappear. Frances came in from school one day, but finding mamma was out making calls, told Nellie that she was going to take her sled and coast down the hill for a while.

"I don't believe your mother would like to

have you stay out to-night, for you have a bad cold," said Nellie.

"Well, I am going to have one more good coast, for the snow is almost gone now."

So Frances went, although knowing it was not the right thing to do. Mrs. Grey came home, but no little girl to welcome her. When it grew dark she felt so very anxious that Ed. was sent to look for her. He at last found her on one of the side streets still coasting, not thinking of the lateness of the hour for her to be away from home, without telling mamma where she was. She felt ashamed and sorry, when she saw how grieved mamma looked; but she did not scold very hard, only said, "I think my little daughter must have forgotten all about my wishes for her health. Your dress is wet, and there is danger of your taking cold."

"Well, it was such fun sliding down the hill, and all the other girls were out."

"I hope you will not have to suffer for exposing yourself, but I am afraid you will."

Mrs. Grey's words proved true, for the next morning poor Frances was sick in bed, with a throbbing head, a high fever, and a voice that was "hoarse as a crow," Ed. said.

Poor child, she now began to think mamma

did know what was best for her. It proved to be quite a severe attack, and Frances was ill for some days. However, with good nursing and constant care she began to improve, and before the week was over was able to sit up, although not to leave her room. Her little friends were very good to come in between school hours and tell her the news.

"I suppose you had the Sewing-Circle just the same, this week?" said Frances to Mary, who was with her one day.

"Yes, we thought it better to sew all we could, so that the poor child might have her clothes."

"Did you have the rehearsal for the tableaux?"

"Well, we had part of it, but you are in all of them, so we couldn't do very much without you. I hope you will be well for next week, and then we can dress the child up, for the things are almost ready. Aunt Fannie says she will help finish up, do the fussy part, like button-holes and putting on belts."

"We mustn't give up the Circle, even after we get that one child dressed up. Mamma says that we can do ever so much good, for there are so many children left alone, without any one to look after them, and sent to homes where they are all taken care of by good people, until they can find friends to be like fathers and mothers to them."

"It is nice to have clothes given, to dress them up neat and clean."

"What a wise girl you are!" said a voice, and in popped Kitty.

The girls had been talking so fast that they didn't know she was so near.

"How are you, Frances?"

"Oh! I am almost well and shall go down-stairs to-morrow."

"I guess you won't want to go coasting again this year."

"No, I don't think I shall. My father said that he guessed winter was about gone."

"Well, we can have just as much fun in the spring, going to picnics and May-parties," said Mary.

"Papa is to spend his vacation in New Hampshire, and we are to board at a hotel."

"Won't that be fun!" said Frances.

"Now we must go home, and you be sure to come to the Sewing-Circle next week."

"Are you going to give the child a bath?"

"Yes, indeed, I am, so you must be there to help," said Mary.

"I wonder what she will say when you tell her?"

"I know I shall laugh when I see her go into the bath-tub," said Kitty.

"Well, you must n't, for then she would think that we were making fun of her, when we only want her to be clean for the new clothes," said Mary.

"We will come to see you to-morrow, Frances, and show you where the lessons will be for Monday," added Kitty.

"I am afraid I shall lose my place in the class by being sick, and I was trying so hard for the diploma," answered she.

After talking for some time longer on various subjects, they at last departed. Wednesday afternoon came, and with it the Sewing-Circle. The girls were all there in season, and with Aunt Fannie's help, the articles of clothing were rapidly finished. She had made the dress and sack; Mary had trimmed a hat quite prettily, a stout pair of boots had been found, and some warm stockings added to the really good outfit.

"Now, girls, I told Bridget Nolan (for that is her name) to be sure to come here at four o'clock, and it is almost time for her to put in an appearance," said Mary.

In a few moments Norah came upstairs, to say that the girl was waiting in the kitchen. Mary quickly ran down to welcome her and bring her to the room, saying to the girls, "Don't laugh."

"Now, Bridget, we want to dress you to-day in the good clothes I told you we were making."

"Yes, miss," she said.

"I am afraid you ought to be washed before we put them on."

"Yes, miss."

"Will you get into the bath-tub, so to be real clean?"

"Yes, miss.

She did indeed look pitiful, so dirty and ragged. Mary was so kind to the poor child that she could not object, but meekly followed her into the bath-room. She seemed to really enjoy this privilege of having a good plunge, and she splashed around vigorously.

The girls had the new clothes ready, and after they all had helped her to dress she stood forth, not a handsome, but a clean, fresh-looking girl.

"Oh! how nice you look! Come and see yourself in the glass," and Mary led her up to the long mirror.

As she caught sight of herself, the look of astonishment plainly showed that she could n't believe it was the same Bridget she had known all her life.

"Now for the hat and sack."

After they had been put on she was all ready for a start.

Mary said, "Now, Bridget, we do n't want you to wear those old clothes any more."

" How can I go begging?"

"You must n't do that, but tell your mother to let you go to school. I will give you the food from here, just the same, but do n't go begging again. Do you want the old clothes?"

"Yes 'm; mother can clane um."

"Why did n't she wash them before?"

"I do n't know, miss."

"Well, do n't you ever wear them again, for they are too dirty and ragged."

"No, miss."

Bridget went away, looking as happy as possible; she, however, took good care to take the bundle with her. The girls afterward found out the reason why she was so eager to keep them.

"She did n't look like the same child after

she had a good wash and some decent clothes on," said Mary.

"I wonder if her mother will make her go begging again?" said Etta.

"Oh! I hope not, for she might be quite a nice girl if she went to school."

"Well, children, you have done your duty, and must wait to see the result, but do n't get discouraged if you fail in this case, but keep on in the work, and you will see good coming in time out of your efforts," said Aunt Fannie.

"I say, girls," put in Hugh, "we must have our show next Saturday afternoon sure; then we can get some more money, if the audience will pay even one cent apiece, so you can buy lots of cloth to sew."

"I wish we could have a little fair now, and make things for that," suggested Annie Bell.

"That 's a fine idea, and we will begin right away, after the tableaux," agreed Mary.

"Your heads will be so full of all this that I am afraid lessons will suffer," said Aunt Fannie.

"Do n't worry, auntie, we always look out for our lessons the very first of all."

Frances came to school one morning, her face beaming with smiles.

"Oh! girls," she cried, "what do you think I have at home?"

"What is it?"

"A darling little baby sister!"

"A real baby?"

"Of course, and we are going to name her Pearl."

"Oh! I want to see her this very day," said Mary.

"I guess you can all have a peep at her in a day or two. She is just lovely, and now I can have fun taking her out in a carriage. Papa asked me this morning if I wanted to see a little stranger, and then he took me into mamma's room, and there she was cuddled down to sleep, with one of her fingers in her mouth. He said, 'Now, Frances, name your little sister.'"

"'Call her Pearl, for she is so lovely!'

"'Indeed, she is a little jewel, and well deserves the pretty name.'"

This little stranger, who had come to them in stormy March, was a great source of pleasure as well as care in the family, and they all loved her very much. The girls made such a pet of the little one, coming to see her every day, admiring all the cunning tricks and ways, which as she grew older were noticed.

Frances just worshipped her, and Ed. could n't help loving the little creature, although he said babies were a bother. This was when his lessons were hard, and she would cry very loud sometimes. So the small stranger soon made friends with all the world about her.

VI.

THE MAY QUEEN.

HE cold March winds had now given way to the warm April breezes and frequent showers, which would cause the grass to spring up and cover the earth with a beautiful new dress, and the trees to bring forth their leaves.

"April showers bring forth May flowers," sang Mary.

" I wish we could have a picnic in our May vacation," Etta said.

"So we can and go out to Longwood."

"How can we go?"

"There is a stage that takes people out there, and we could go to a grove near a house which papa owns, take our dinner, and stay all day," replied Mary.

"We 'll have a gorgeous time!"

"We must have our tableaux first, so to get money for the fair."

"When will that be?"

"Not until fall, then we can work all summer and ask our friends to help us."

'"What children you are, always planning to do so many things! I am afraid you can never accomplish half," said Mrs. Grey. They were in her room, so she was hearing all the plans.

"Oh! yes, we will, and lots besides. We are working hard in school, for our examination will come soon. I have all my lessons, which I lost when I was sick, to make up," said Frances.

"It will be too bad if you do n't get a diploma."

"Well, I am going to study just as hard as I can, but my arithmetic keeps me back, it is so puzzling."

"Frances will feel satisfied that she has done her best, even if she fails in receiving a diploma," answered mamma.

So the days and weeks went by, and it was almost the first of May. The young people of Mr. Grey's church always held a May-day party. Like the Christmas festival, they prepared songs, recitations, and dialogues, all about "lovely spring" instead of the cold winter.

When they were not in school or preparing their lessons, they found plenty to take up their time. Now the next important event was the grand entertainment, or "show," as the young manager, Hugh, called it. Word was given out to the boys and girls who wished to see the wonderful performance, to come on Saturday afternoon, with *one cent* as the price of admission.

At the time mentioned, a crowd of children was ready to view the scene.

"Why, Frances, ever so many have come!" said Etta, as she drew the curtain aside and peeped out into the larger room.

"Now, girls, are you ready? The French Spy is coming first, and you must be at the table when the curtain goes up; hurry and get your caps on, and remember to clink the glasses together when I give the sign! Keep your eyes on me, and you can't make a mistake." These instructions Hugh gave by jerks, as he rushed about to get all in working order.

"I feel rather shaky," said Frances.

"I know I shall laugh the very first thing," said Etta.

"How do I look in this scarlet dress?" said Kitty.

"As gorgeous as a tulip," said Charlie Howard.

"Do n't flatter, sir, but see that the curtain is all right to pull back."

"Never fear, it goes like magic."

"Clear the stage; it is time to begin, for they are all clapping! Take your places at the table, girls, and don't laugh; look at each other and not at the folks, and remember the sign when to clink!"

The bell rang, and after numerous hitches of the curtain, it was pulled aside, and the impatient audience were given a glimpse of the wonders within.

Frances and Etta were seen seated at a table, on which were a number of glasses. They looked very pretty in their fancy dresses and white caps. But, alas! Etta had said "she should laugh," and just as Hugh gave the sign for them to raise their glasses, she began to shake with laughter, her glass struck against the one Frances held, — a crash! — and both fell in pieces on the table. The audience joined with the performers in a hearty laugh, and the curtain fell in the midst of confusion.

"Well, Etta, you just spoiled that scene," Hugh said with a frown, although he was laughing himself. "Now for Cinderella! Frances, you get ready as soon as you can, for they do n't like to wait."

In a few moments she appeared in a white

dress, trimmed with roses, a pretty blue sash, and her hair in waves over her shoulders. ˑ

"You must bob your hair up and slip on this old dress. I 've got a string tied to the hem, and when it is time, I 'll pull it off; then you must untie the handkerchief on your head so it will drop on the floor. Now we are ready! Charlie, pull the string when I ring the bell. Stop laughing, Kitty! You must look haughty at Cinderella. This is Scene One — Cinderella sitting in the ashes, and the unkind sisters going to the ball!"

"Poor little thing!"

"Look at her rags!"

"Oh! how fine the sisters look!"

Thus the excited children talked, as the pictures or tableaux were placed before them.

"This is Scene Two, where the Fairy Godmother touches Cinderella with her magic wand, and she goes to the ball."

The picture was again the poor ragged child, but lo! in a minute, at one touch of the fairy-wand, the old dress has been changed into a lovely white dress, covered with roses and ribbons, and the slipshod boots into tiny white slippers. Frances looked just as sweet as a blush-rose in June. Her cheeks grew pink, and her eyes bright. Then Hugh threw the red light over the scene.

"Is n't it fine?"

"How do you suppose she got the old clothes off so quickly?"

"Oh! I know," said one of the boys. "Hugh had a string tied to the dress, and could pull it without our seeing him."

"Now, here is Scene Three. The Prince has come to have the haughty sisters try on the little slipper, which some lady lost at the ball. They each try to wear the slipper, but it is too small, although they pinch their toes to get it on. Cinderella is in rags, but the Prince tells her to try it on. Lo! it just fits her! The Fairy Godmother appears, and the lovely lady, whom the Prince saw at the ball, comes back. It is Cinderella, but so changed that the haughty sisters hardly know her. The Prince chooses her for his bride!"

Then the red light glows over the really pretty picture, and the curtain is drawn, amidst loud applause and a general choking, caused by burning the powder.

Charlie Howard steps out before the audience and says, "That will be all to-day, but we will have some more next week."

Such a chattering as was heard when the children left the play-room to go home! They all agreed "it was fine, and that they would come to see the next performance."

"I tell you, girls, that was a big success, and they all liked it first-rate," said Charlie Howard.

"Well, Etta spoiled The French Spy by laughing, and I told her to be careful."

"*You* looked so comical, with that funny cap on, and the moustache made you look so fierce, that I could n't help laughing."

"Never mind, the rest was so good that it did n't spoil the whole thing," said Mary, who was always a peace-maker.

This occasion was only the beginning of a series of similar ones, and they were always sure of a crowd of spectators.

"Now we will count the money. Bring it here, Frankie, and let 's add up."

Frank Bliss, who was doorkeeper, brought forward the box, and much to their surprise thirty cents were counted.

"Only think, to get all that the first time! We can make ever so much more before the long vacation."

"I am going to get moss and ferns to make pictures for the fair, when I am in the country this summer. Mamma says the little acorn-cups can be made into perfume bouquets. She will show me how to fix them," said Frances.

"We must all think of every thing that is pretty to make for our fair, for we want it to be very nice," said Etta.

"Well, Mary, you keep all the money we get," said Kitty.

" I 'll be the money-keeper," she answered.

The most interesting pleasure of the Spring festival was choosing a May Queen, who at that time was crowned with a wreath of flowers. A great honor it was to be chosen, and hearts beat with anxiety until the choice had been made. This year it was to be decided at the singing-school, who should be Queen of the May. They whispered among themselves about this one and that.

One of the girls said, " I think Frances Grey ought to be chosen this year, for she has never been a Queen."

The other girls agreed heartily in this, so Frances was to have that honor.

A dialogue, " The May Queen," was to be prepared, and Frances had a long speech to learn, which she was to repeat after being crowned. This was an easy thing for her to do; "she could do any thing but arithmetic," she said.

She burst into the house that evening, shouting, "Oh! mamma, I 'm to be Queen, and now you must make my white dress, and I want a new light blue sash and some pretty slippers and——"

"My dear child, do not add any more to the list, for I am afraid poor mamma will have as much as she can do to get ready all that you have named."

"Is n't it lovely to think I was chosen?"

"Yes, it shows that my little daughter is loved by her friends. Remember, if we are kind and gentle, our companions will always remember us with affection."

"There are some children I do n't like, but I try to be kind to them even if they are rude."

"The example of a polite child has great influence on those who are rough in their manners, so that after a while they will drop the rude way, when they see the difference," said Mrs. Grey.

Annie Bell's mamma was so ill that she was not able to keep house, so they boarded very near where Frances lived. The daughter of the house, Rosa, had a piano and was a very nice musician. Annie had begun to take music lessons of her. Frances was very fond of going to see Annie, and also to listen to Rosa, who would kindly play for them.

I wish I could learn how to play, it must be just lovely," she said one day.

"I will give you lessons if you will practise every day," replied Rosa.

"Why, I have n't a piano, so I can't take lessons, but I should like to ever so much."

"Would you be willing to come here to use my piano?"

"Oh! yes, indeed, and I will ask mamma this evening."

"Annie can practise one hour at noon, and you can come after school at night."

"I 'm so glad, for now perhaps I can play as well as Mary does sometime."

So this was a very important question to be settled, and Frances eagerly set forth all the advantages to be gained.

"Only think, papa, perhaps I can learn so as to play well enough for the Sunday school. How I wish I had a piano myself!"

"Perhaps if you are patient, it will come in due time like the skates."

"Well, I always have to wait for every thing;

now Mary can have just what she wants right away."

"My daughter must remember that we are not rich people, and so can not have all the luxuries at once. I do n't think there is a doubt but that you may possess a piano some day, if you show that you are really in earnest about the music lessons."

"Then you are willing I should begin this week?"

"Yes, my dear, and all I ask is that you prove faithful to the work and improve as fast as possible "

"Now I may play as well as Mary does sometime. I am going to try any way."

So Rosa began the lessons with Frances, who daily went to her home to practise the five-finger exercises, and learn to read the notes quickly and correctly. This was a source of great pleasure and profit to her. Her first thought now was, as she often said, "to play as nice as Mary does." She always thought that Mary was almost perfect in every thing she did, and she in her turn said that Frances "was too *sweet* for any thing." The affection between these friends was very charming, and they seemed almost like sisters.

It was near May-day, and the children were eagerly waiting, hoping it would be pleasant, for there was much enjoyment in prospect. A number of kind people always planned for this holiday and for the children who wished to join in the amusements, and Music Hall was open for them to carry out the entertainment.

In the morning they would meet, and then barges and carriages were ready to take the girls and little ones to ride; the boys and older ones forming into line and marching to the music of the band, which went with them. At last they reached Music Hall, where pleasant games and a social time, with plenty of cake and ice-cream, were enjoyed by all. A very pretty sight to see the girls dressed in white, trimmed with ribbons and flowers, each carrying a little flag of red, white, and blue, which they waved as they went along the crowded streets.

The good man who had planned all this enjoyment, and with the help of others carried it out, looked as pleased as any little child, his kindly face beaming with smiles as he watched the young folks.

The girls were talking in Aunt Fannie's room, about going to this festival. "I do n't believe I can go, for I am May Queen that very evening, and I know mamma will think I shall get too tired, if I go to both places," said Frances.

"We might go a little while in the morning, and you can rest in the afternoon," answered Mary.

"I know aunt won't let me go, for she says I am never at home, and that we play too much," said Etta.

"Well, I think it is quite true; it is nice to play, but we should be willing to work and make ourselves useful," said Aunt Fannie's gentle voice.

"Oh! we must all go this time sure, for it will be great fun," Kitty added.

"I can't be in the procession any way, for my mamma said so," put in Annie Bell.

"Well, never mind the procession, but we will go to the hall, and see them dance around the May-pole and crown the Queen."

"That's so, girls; what's the use of staying at home when every one is going?" and Hugh's voice was heard at the door.

"Well, I will tease aunt so hard she will have to let me go," Etta said very earnestly.

"I'll help you, and I know she can't resist us both," offered Kitty.

"Here's a little Queen," Mary shouted, twirling Frances round; "won't she look pretty with her new white dress and the crown upon her head?"

"You are a duck!" "Well, you are a dumpling, so fat and round!"

"Girls, stop your fooling and come upstairs to the play-room," said the boys, "and we will play blind-man's buff by numbers."

Aunt Fannie said to grandpa, as she heard their merry voices, "Dear children, how happy they are. May their lives be always bright!"

"Yes, they are a busy lot of little ones, never still a moment."

"Their spirits are just bubbling over all the time. Let them play while they can, for the cares come soon enough."

So said the older ones, as the echo of the joyous laughter rang through the house. Meanwhile school duties must be kept in order, and now they were reviewing the studies, ready for examinations, before vacation.

"Oh, dear!" Frances said, after working hard on some examples, which at last proved wrong. "I wish arithmetic had never been invented."

Papa laughed. "So might we say of every thing which it was hard for us to learn."

"Well, what good is it, only to bother!"

"It helps to train the mind, makes us correct in thought, and is used in business life."

"I don't think it helps my mind, for I am all upset every time I try to do the sums right and they come wrong," said Frances, impatiently.

"That very effort is doing you good, although you don't think so."

"Oh! but I do love history, and I can remember dates real well. I could study it all day."

"Well, my dear, you have a great deal of pleasure before you, in finding out the events which have brought us to this very day and hour."

"I think it is splendid to learn about Columbus, and how he sailed away from Spain, not knowing where he should find land again."

"A brave man, who did a wonderful work in finding this great country. Thus you see by his life what thought and study did for him."

"How kind Queen Isabella was to sell her jewels, so that he might have the money to use!"

"Yes, a noble woman can do much good in the world, if only by her influence."

"I don't believe I shall ever do any great thing."

"My daughter must remember that only a very few people do that, but we can all live good and pure lives from day to day, which is really a wonderful thing, when we think of all the temptations we have to encounter, and what we have to learn from childhood. Have your aim high, my dear, and strive to do every thing in your power to be a true woman. Improve the hours and fit yourself to be of use in the world."

"I wish I could write poetry, but I never can."

Papa laughed.

"You fanciful child, always wishing to do something odd! I think you write very nice compositions for a little girl, and that is quite a hard task, to arrange one's thoughts in a proper form."

Papa and Frances often had these little talks, which they both enjoyed. Mr. Grey said to his wife, "Frances is a very sensible child, but full of desires, which, although now beyond her, may, if rightly directed, be of great benefit to her as she grows older."

May - day came, warm and pleasant; the Common had put on its new spring dress of lovely green, the fresh new leaves on the trees had appeared, the little birds were building their nests among the boughs of the tall elm trees, twittering to each other of the warm summer which was soon to come. The broad malls reaching out in every direction, and the pond sparkling in the sunlight, made a beautiful picture for the people to enjoy, as they went to and fro, intent on their various duties. These busy people, however, stopped to gaze on the bright faces and sparkling eyes of the young folks, who went by in the procession, *their* whole thought being on pleasure. Sometimes a sigh would escape from one of the girls, whose life was spent in a close workroom, wishing that she was once more a child free from care. The smiles and cheers of these happy children, however, echoed in her mind all day, and she felt better for just seeing the joy of their young life.

Music Hall had become almost a home to the children, so many happy hours were spent within its walls. This day was to be a pleasure from beginning to end. Mary and her friends were all there in season to see the May-pole march, and the crowning of the pretty Queen. Then they all marched "Lady Walpole's March," boys and girls together. It was great fun, and at the end a company of breathless children were given time to rest before another march was in order.

As Frances must go home before afternoon, she reluctantly parted from the others.

" I much rather have stayed and had a good time with the children, than to be the May Queen to-night," Frances said.

" You must remember that you will be giving pleasure to others in thus helping," mamma answered.

" Well, it is nice to be the Queen, and I wish I could look as pretty as the one I saw this morning."

" I think you will do very nicely ; be natural and like your own self; that will be beauty enough."

" Oh! how I wish I could be handsome!"

" Did you ever hear this: Handsome is as handsome does ? "

" Mary is *so pretty* that every one looks at her, and the other day a lady said, 'What a lovely girl!' as we were passing along. I know she didn't mean any one but Mary."

Mrs. Grey laughed. " Perhaps she might have meant Kitty, or Etta, or Annie, for they are *all* pretty girls."

"No, for she touched Mary's curls as she said it."

Frances did not think herself that she was a very sweet-looking child and would make a pretty woman. Thus this very idea made her all the more attractive.

The evening soon came, and Frances at last was dressed, although mamma thought she was rather fussy and hard to suit. She seemed satisfied with the result, as well she might be, for she looked like a little fairy in her gauzy white dress, looped with May-flowers, and a bouquet of the same to carry in her hand. The girls, of course, shared a sight of her and were loud in their praises. They were to go to the festival as invited guests.

"You look just like a rose-bud," said one.

"Won't you feel grand, when they put on the crown?"

"You are going to live with the fairies to-night, but come back to us to-morrow."

"Stop! you foolish girls, or I shall forget all I know, and I feel *trembly* now, when I think of it."

"We must go, as it is almost seven o'clock, but don't you make me laugh, for I certainly shall if you look comical at me," said Frances.

"No, we will be as sober as we can, so the little darling sha'n't forget her speech."

The large audience-room was crowded with the children and their parents. The platform looked very bright and pretty, covered with pot-plants, and garlands of flowers twined around the pictures and hanging from the gas fixtures. A throne had been built, with flowers all about it, on which the Queen was to rest. A number of songs and recitations were given by the children, even the little ones repeating some verse about the spring-time.

Then the May Queen was to be presented. All was excitement, until the group of fairies was seen upon the stage, and then it grew quiet, as they each told what good work they had done to weary mortals, who needed a kind touch and a helping hand. They had come back to their fairy-home to tell the good Queen of this; were to hold a festival, and again crown her as their loved leader.

One of the fairies stepping forward said, "Here comes our beauteous Queen!"

Then all repeated, "All hail!" as she came in view. Two fairy-sisters took her by the hand, led her to the throne or bower, while another placed a beautiful crown upon her head. A joyous song then burst forth from all. The Queen rose and thanked her subjects for the honor, asked them to tell her of any good done to poor suffering creatures. They did as she bade them, and with a smile she said, " It is well, go on with your mission; the reward of doing a kind act is far greater than wearing a crown."

She then joined the group, and clasping hands they sang a beautiful tribute to her goodness and wisdom. Thus ended the pretty scene, amidst great applause, which called again for the last song.

It had been a success, and the girls might well feel proud of their effort. Frances was indeed a "lovely Queen " and well sustained her part. She had felt very timid before going on the stage, wishing herself anywhere else, but she grew brave and went through her duty perfectly, and as all who took part had been so well trained, the whole was very smoothly done.

The lovely spring days sped away, each bringing some new pleasure to those who love the bursting forth of beautiful Nature. The Common was a source of joy to all those privileged to enjoy its beauties. Again the children made it a playground almost every moment of leisure, and a happy company could be seen sitting under the shade of the noble trees, or walking on the broad paths with their doll children, to keep company with the real babies, who daily visited with their nurses this lovely spot.

Just opposite the Common stood an old-fashioned stone house, known as the "Hancock House," belonging to the family of that name, which from earliest colonial times had been noted in Boston. It was set back from the street, surrounded by a garden, in front of which was a fence not very high, with a gate by which to enter the grounds. This garden was filled with shrubs of different kinds, the lilacs, syringa, and fine roses; in one corner was a large bed of lily of the valley, and many other plants found a home in this quiet spot. It was a picture of comfort, and in the spring-time, when the shrubs were in blossom, a "bower of beauty." The children daily walked by, and would peep into the garden with longing eyes, wishing they could have some of the fragrant blossoms.

One day, as they had thus stopped to gaze, Kitty ran up the steps to gain a nearer view, when a gentleman, who was walking in the path, turned quickly to see the person, and when it proved to be only a blue-eyed girl, he smiled pleasantly, saying, "What is it, my little girl?"

Kitty was so taken aback that she could only stammer, "I was only looking, sir."

"Won't you and your friends walk in to see the flowers?"

"Oh! thank you, sir."

So they at last found themselves within the beautiful enclosure. This gentleman of the honored name was tall and dignified-looking, with iron gray hair and a stately manner, but he spoke kindly to them, and after they had explored the garden filled their hands full of the sweet flowers. He inquired their names and, when he found that they were almost neighbors, asked them to come again, every day if they wished, as long as the flowers lasted.

Mary, who could always say the right thing, thanked him for the invitation and the flowers.

This was a great treat to them, and often were their eager faces and bright eyes seen at the gate, waiting for their friend to appear.

"I wish I could live always in that lovely old house," said Frances.

' Would n't it be fun to have a play-room

away up where those windows are on the roof, and look out upon the trees waving their branches?" said Annie Bell.

This estate was indeed a charming landmark of the early days of Boston. The very atmosphere about it seemed to tell of the wisdom which had dwelt within its walls. The old mansion stood there many years, but with the march of time it had to give way to more spacious dwellings. Two brownstone mansions stand on the spot, lifting their walls up to the very sky, it would almost seem. To these children's hearts it was a fragrant memory, and always a new pleasure of their girlhood.

THE HANCOCK HOUSE.

VII.

THE SUMMER VACATION.

THE school examinations were now in order. The children worked hard to have them as nearly perfect as possible. One day geography was the study to review. Frances had taken a bad cold in her head, and every moment her eyes were filled with tears, as the girls thought who noticed this, thinking that she could not answer the questions.

"Why, Frances," said one after school, "what made you cry so much? I do n't think the questions were very hard."

"What an idea! I was n't *crying;* it was only a cold in my head made my eyes run. If it had been the arithmetic I should certainly have wept."

She always felt like crying when her bright ideas flew away, and she labored so hard with this study. Poor Annie Bell's hardest task was spelling, and she always had the lowest per cent. for this study. Thus it is with both old and young, — some one thing seems to be so laborious, while others are really a pleasure. So with these friends; they all had ability, but certain studies were hard for them. However, they received high marks in these examinations.

Miss French was much pleased at the result. She felt troubled, however, in her mind, for a decision must be made who should receive the four diplomas to be given in her class, and it was hard to make a choice. She must look over the records carefully, and it would depend on the credit

FANEUIL HALL.

for conduct and attendance, as well as for examinations. She knew how hard her pupils had tried to gain the reward, and wished to make a just decision. Whoever was chosen, they would all know that she showed no favor.

During these days the children still had their pleasures. The State House was just opposite the Common, at the head of Park street. It is a noble building, dear to the hearts of Boston people, and admired by all visitors for its substantial appearance. How many stirring words and eloquent speeches have been made within its walls! It was a favorite amusement for these friends to make a journey to the very top of the building, and view from this height the scene spread before them. They were often seen running up the numerous steps which lead from the street to the grand entrance, making their way to the steep and narrow flight of stairs which brought them to the dome above. These stairs were winding, and they arrived at the top, dizzy and all out of breath. Then they would look from the small windows, trying to count the boats in the harbor. They could see from here the city clustering around this beacon light; the harbor full of vessels of all sizes and descriptions, from the stately foreign steamship to the small row-boat; the distant islands on which a number of the city's public buildings are placed, and beyond the bay broadening out as far as the eye could reach. Also could be seen the beautiful suburbs of Boston, nestling among the green trees, and venerable Bunker Hill monument, raising its proud head to the blue sky above. It was a

city to be proud of, and these children unconsciously were learning to love and be loyal to
their noble home. In future years, wherever
they might be, the memory would be ever fresh
and bright, of these childhood pleasures and of
Boston city.

Hugh would say, "Look over there, as far as
you can, and see that line of smoke: it is a
steamer coming up the bay; we shall soon see
more of it, and then the vessel will come in
view."

"It seems as if the water and sky are very
near together."

"Yes, but you know the geography says the
earth is round, and that makes the top of the
vessel come in sight first."

"If it was evening we could see the Boston
revolving light."

"Look at that tiny sail-boat spinning along."

"It seems as if the sails were dipping into
the water."

"I should be afraid to be so near the big
waves."

"Now, girls, look! that is a foreign steamer.
I know by the leaning smoke-stack."

"Oh! how I wish I could sail away some day!
I would like to be a sailor boy."

So they talked as the picture changed before their gaze, showing that the lessons they had learned were not forgotten. Did the patter of little feet and the echo of the young voices reach the ears of the wise fathers, as they were assembled in the rooms below, considering the laws of the State?

The Sewing-Circle and the tableaux still claimed attention, and more money was added to the fund for the fair from time to time. Bridget Nolan was also remembered, and the children often spoke a kindly word when she came to Mary's house for food. They noticed that at first she wore the clothes which had been made for her. One day, however, as they were crossing the street on their way to the Common, Mary exclaimed, "Why, girls, is n't that Bridget going around the corner?"

"What, that girl in those ragged clothes?"

"Yes, it looks like her."

"Hurry up, so we can see her face before she gets round the corner."

"She sees us and is almost running."

"Then it is she, and she is ashamed."

It was Bridget, and she "sneaked away," so Hugh said, out of sight as soon as possible.

"Now, is n't it too bad that she should wear

those horrible old clothes again? I suppose her mother made her go begging, and thought she would get more if she looked as poor as possible," said Mary.

" Well, Aunt Fannie told us not to get discouraged if we could n't do much good for her, but keep on trying to help people."

" Perhaps she do n't want to beg, poor child."

" Papa, what do you think? That child we dressed so nice is out in her old clothes begging again."

" Is that so? When did you see her?"

" To-day for the first time."

" Poor child, she must have unkind parents to compel her to go around asking charity in that way."

" Perhaps her father and mother are dead, and those with whom she lives treat her thus," said mamma.

" She would n't tell us *just* where she lived, only said 'near a wharf.'"

" That was not very definite, and I presume she did n't want visitors going to the place. I often see these wretched homes in my walks, where the living is not obtained by fair means. So we must not blame the girl too harshly," said Mr. Grey.

"Mary says she shall speak to her about it, the very next time she comes to the house. I am afraid she never will be able to catch her again, for she knows Mary would n't like it. Perhaps her folks have sold the clothes and oblige her to wear the ragged ones. We thought she was very anxious to take them away. She did n't mean for us to see her, for she knew we told her not to wear those rags again," said Frances.

This going back of Bridget to her old ways was rather a hard thing for the girls to bear, and their zeal lagged somewhat in the good work. Aunt Fannie told them that often in life, when we had done our very best for people, they would prove ungrateful, but that the only way was to try again, and the reward would come sooner or later.

" Well, we shall have the Sewing-Circle just the same, and give the clothes to some mission, then we shall know they will do good."

Frances told the girls what her papa said, and the interest was renewed, the meetings being kept up until vacation. When they were all together one day, Hugh asked, "Girls, when are we going to have our picnic?"

"The first holiday."

"Well, the only one we have this month is the Seventeenth of June."

"That will be next week."

"We can plan for that day, there is time enough."

Of course the fathers and mothers were to be consulted, as the necessary pocket money must be their contribution for the good time, and also for the luncheons. As they were willing, the plans were made, and quite a number of children were invited to join the party. The sun arose brightly on the morning of the day, but soon went into a cloud.

"A sure sign of rain," Ed. said, as Frances was hurrying to get ready to go.

"Do you think it will rain, mamma?"

"I hope not, for I should not let you go if I thought it would rain. Are you going with them, Ed.?"

"No; I guess you do n't find me at any such little picnic!"

"Perhaps you may learn, my son, that life is made up of small pleasures, and that the lesser joys help us to enjoy the greater."

"Well, I do n't like a girls' picnic."

Mrs. Grey laughed. "Oh! Ed., you are a

queer boy, but you may change your ideas as
you grow older."

At last all was ready, and the children met
at the corner from which the stage was to start,
—a merry group, looking so fresh and bright,
carrying their luncheon baskets full of goodies.
They were soon on the way, Hugh and Frankie
Bliss riding with the driver; down Beacon
street with its fine residences, past the Common
and Public Garden, out to the Mill-dam with
its broad carriage road. To the right, the
Charles river was sparkling in the morning sun,
which now was shining over all the scene.

After quite a long ride they entered Longwood, with its fine roads shaded by trees,
elegant houses surrounded by lovely grounds,
—homes of the rich. It is a charming place
and a favorite drive for the city people, also
visitors, who say that it looks "very English."

The children were aware that the stopping-
place had been reached, by a shout from Hugh
saying, "Stop! here we are; unload your passengers!"

The boys scrambled down from the top of the
stage, and the girls were soon with them.

"We will go home with you this afternoon,

please meet us at this place," said Mary to the driver.

"All right, miss, I 'll be here at four o'clock."

They followed Hugh, who led the way to a pretty grove, quite a distance from the road. After putting the luncheon baskets in a place of safety, they began to plan what should be done for amusement. They had brought "ring toss" with them, and a merry game they played for an hour. Then the boys proposed a walk, but the girls thought it was almost time to get dinner.

"You can take a stroll while we fix things for the feast," said Mary.

"See if you can find any berries."

"I do n't believe many grow about here; one must go out into the *real* country for those."

"We 'll have every thing ready by the time you come back."

So they chatted, their young voices making music in the grove.

"I have brought a table-cloth, and we will lay it down on the grass," said Mary.

"The black ants will run over the food," said Etta.

"Do n't get it out until the boys come back."

"We can make wreaths of these maple leaves and trim our hats with them."

" That 's so, and then every one will know we have been to a picnic."

Before long they heard the boys shouting to each other, and then they appeared in view, their hands full of white daisies and buttercups.

"Oh! how lovely! we can make such pretty bouquets of them."

" Dinner all ready?"

"We 'll have it, now you have come back."

"I 'm so hungry I could eat the world up!"

The table was soon set on the grass, and the children were quickly disposing of the treat. The friendly ants, wasps, a number of spiders, and also worms, kept them company, trying to get their share of the goodies. The day had been quite warm and pleasant, but now dark clouds came in the sky, and distant thunder was heard.

"Oh! there is going to be a thunder shower!"

"We must pack up these things as quick as we can, and go down to the house before it rains."

"That 's so, girls, we shall have to hurry, for it is coming nearer."

"I'm dreadfully afraid of thunder and lightning!"

"All I care about is getting wet through."

"There, do n't stop to talk, but go right off."

So they scrabbled up their baskets, collected shawls and hats, but before they could start a loud peal of thunder and a sharp flash of lightning came.

"We shall have to run for it," said Hugh.

They did indeed have to run, and the rain came down in torrents just before they reached the shelter of the house.

"It was lucky we came as soon as we did, or we should have been like drowned rats," said Kitty.

"I guess my mother will worry about me. Ed. said it would rain, for the sun went into a cloud," added Frances.

It proved to be not only a shower, but a regular rain, and all they could do was to stay in the shelter, and wait for the stage to take them home. It was nearly four o'clock, but the stage did not appear.

"I think, girls, we shall have to walk to the next corner to catch it," said Hugh.

It was as he said, and the children scampered as fast as possible, reaching the corner just in time to stop the stage. The ride home was not so pleasant as it had been in the morning. It was raining hard and was so muddy that the windows had to be closed. This made it so hot and close that Frances and Kitty were "seasick," as they said, and at last were obliged to keep their heads out of the windows, Frances on one side, and Kitty on the other. Although feeling just as miserable as they possibly could, they could n't help laughing at themselves, in which all the children joined.

At last they reached the end of the route, a rather forlorn-looking company, tired and wet, but the wreaths on their hats and the pretty bouquets of wild flowers told that they had been to a picnic, and it was no wonder they came home tired after a day spent in the woods. Ed. was waiting with an umbrella for Frances.

"Well, here you are at last; I guess your mother will scold you for staying out in the rain!"

"I could n't help it, we had to wait for the stage."

"We've had a jolly time to-day; had company, and ice-cream for dinner."

This was too much for Frances; she burst

out crying, which she continued until the house was reached.

"Why, my darling, .what is the matter?" cried mamma.

"Ed. said you were going to scold me. I couldn't come any sooner, and I was sick in the stage, and you had ice-cream, and, oh! dear, I wish I hadn't gone."

"I am very sorry, Ed., that you should tease your little sister when she is tired. You knew I was only anxious when the shower came up so suddenly, and didn't blame her."

"Well, I didn't think she would cry for *that*. Don't feel bad, sis, I was only fooling."

After a little while she stopped crying, but mamma thought the best place for her was in bed, as it had been hard work hunting after pleasure. Ed. loved his sister, but couldn't resist the temptation of "bossing her" sometimes. His mother talked seriously to him of this fault, and showed him how unkind it really was to wound the feelings of others, if he was only in fun.

"Frances never can stand any thing."

"The more reason, then, why you should favor her," said Mrs. Grey.

Ed. thought then that he would always be

kind to his little sister, but he found that the feeling to "just tease her a little" would come into his mind, and he had to fight, to conquer the enemy.

So ended the Seventeenth of June picnic. The next morning found the children rather tired, but ready to go to school. It was now nearing vacation very rapidly, and Miss French had planned to have the last day devoted to reading and singing. The diplomas were to be given out, that day, and the girls were all excitement to know who should be the fortunate ones to receive them.

"I wonder if *I* shall get a diploma!" said Frances almost every day.

"Time will prove," answered papa.

"Well, I have held a good rank, only when I was sick, and perhaps that will not make much difference. There are six girls who keep together in the class, and it will be hard to choose."

"Don't think too much about it, my dear."

"I can't help it, for I have set my heart on getting one."

"It is not wise to do so, for you may be disappointed," replied papa.

Wednesday was to be the closing day, so the

children were only to go to school in the morning. The parents were invited to visit the school if they wished. Mrs. Grey could not leave baby Pearl, so was not present. Quite a number of visitors came in to hear the scholars read. They all showed much improvement, and it was an enjoyable exercise.

At the close Miss French said that she would present diplomas to the four scholars who had received the highest marks in their studies, conduct, and attendance ; she also said that it had been difficult to decide, as a number of them had kept so closely together in rank, that really six should receive rewards, but as four was the number to be given, the scholars who had been absent or tardy only *once* during the school year were entitled to the diplomas.

A silence followed after she had spoken. Frances felt her heart beat quickly, but as Miss French continued she thought of her absence in the winter. Then as she named the scholars, all doubt was over. She called the names of Mary Swan, Julia, Shaw, Ada Green, and Etta Kendall, and they went forward to the desk to receive the prizes.

Poor Frances! it was a great disappointment; tears came into her eyes, but she bravely held them back, knowing that it was really her own fault that she had been sick and obliged to be away from school, but it did not make her feel a bit better. The girls pitied her, for they knew how much she had longed for the diploma. As she entered the house and went into mamma's room, who saw at once that her little girl was in a sad state of mind, she did not say a word for a few moments, but at last her grief burst forth.

"I will never *try* for *any thing* again as long ——" but her sobs stopped her.

"My dear child, don't feel so badly, but tell mamma all about it," and she drew the little girl into her lap, soothing her grief.

"I didn't get it, just because I was absent. I thought Mary would have one, but I didn't think Etta would get one instead of me."

The sobs burst forth again.

"Isn't Etta your dear friend?"

"Yes, but I wanted the diploma!"

"Can't you feel glad for her success?"

"No, I can't; there was only a little difference between us, but Miss French gave it to her, even after I made up all my lessons."

"But my dear, your absence counted against you."

"I know it, but I do n't think it is fair.   It is no use trying for any thing."

"Perhaps my darling will see that she is rather hasty in her thought, after a little while. *Try* to overcome this feeling which is now troubling you, and you will be glad for your friend."

But Frances could not at present feel any better. She was so disappointed that a feeling of anger against her teacher, and of envy for Etta's success, was uppermost in her mind. Of course this made her very unhappy, and deeply grieved. Mamma felt sorry for her child, missing her usually sunshiny daughter. It was a hard time for all, as "the girls," knowing how deeply she felt, hardly knew what to say to comfort her.

Mamma said to them, "It is much better not to talk about it at present. I think Frances will see that Miss French could do no other way, as it stood."

It was a bitter lesson for Frances, but away down in her heart she knew that her disobedience to mamma's wishes had caused the sickness which kept her away from school. She knew that Miss French had been very kind about it, but of course could not change the marks. She fought against these feelings of anger and envy and at last conquered.

"I think, mamma, I do begin to feel a little bit glad for Etta."

"I thought you would, my dear. You know, poor Etta does not have quite so many blessings as you do, with no father or mother to love her."

"I know it, and she did work hard for it. I have n't wanted to see her since, but now I feel differently. Can I invite her to spend the day with me before we go away?"

"Certainly, my dear, and you must be doubly kind to her, for she has known your feeling about the decision."

So Frances went to Etta's home and gained permission to have her for a day. Frances felt much happier after she had talked her trouble over, and had put her arms about Etta's neck and kissed her, saying "that she was glad to have her get the diploma," but she added, "I did want it *dreadfully*."

"I know you were disappointed, but I could n't help it."

"Well, never mind now. I do n't feel quite so badly about it as I did."

So this ripple on the surface of their friendship was subdued and never again appeared.

The children were all to spend the vacation in the country, and great preparations were necessary to accomplish this plan. Brother Ed. was to stay with Aunt Mira, so he could catch woodchucks, wear his old clothes, go barefooted, and have a jolly time. He did n't want to stay in a hotel dressed up. He therefore departed, and the rest of the family were to start in a few days. The girls had made many promises to write to each other *every day.*

A pleasant morning found Mr. Grey and Mrs. Grey, with Frances and little Pearl, at the depot, ready to join the party of friends who were to go with them. Frances was impatient to have the time come to be moving. The gong sounded, and they were soon on their way to the hills of New Hampshire.

At last the city was left far behind, and they just flew past villages, stopping only at the large towns. Frances employed the time at first in looking out of the window, viewing all the sights, but they went so fast that when she would say, "Oh! mamma, look at that pretty brook!" it would be left far behind. Then she tried to count the cows in the pastures, but could hardly get beyond one, when away the train would go past them.

"I wish it would n't go so fast," she said.

"I think you will be glad, before we get to our stopping-place, to have the distance so quickly gained," answered mamma.

It was a merry party who were to make their home together for the coming weeks; they laughed and chatted, talking of the pleasures they expected to enjoy during this summer trip. At twelve o'clock the lunch-baskets were in demand, and cold meat, bread and butter, and boiled eggs were soon disposed of.

After lunch Frances began to feel sleepy, and was soon taking a nap, keeping company with little Pearl. When she woke up she thought it must be home, until the jar and rumble of the cars told the story.

"Are we almost there, mamma?"

"Not quite."

"Oh! I wish we were."

This she repeated after every little "cat nap," in which she indulged at intervals. All the party echoed the wish, as the afternoon wore on and they began to be tired of whirling along, feeling hot and dusty. At last the welcome sound of "Franklin!" was heard.

Picking up bags and bundles they quickly alighted, glad to be able to walk about once more. The stage, however, was waiting to take them to the hotel. The genial landlord was there to welcome them, and a pretty girl showed them to their rooms.

Oh! how comfortable it all was, and how nice to be able to shake off the dust and wash in the fresh water. In a short time the bell rang out its welcome sound, and they found tea awaiting them in the cool dining-room; the white bread and golden butter, the luscious field strawberries, fresh and sweet, tasted so nice.

After tea the piazza must be visited, and the lovely view of mountain and valley, in the midst a broad river reflecting the rays of the golden sun, which was just setting behind the tallest peak, was a beautiful sight to enjoy, before the twilight crept over it.

As Mr. Grey said, "It rested one's body and mind to be able to see such a scene. God was so good to his children, in giving them these glorious sights, with health to enjoy his blessings."

The friends about him thought that the prospect of enjoying the vacation time was well begun, and went to rest, satisfied with their new surroundings.

The next morning Frances awoke bright and early. She quickly dressed, ran downstairs to see some children who were running on the piazza, laughing and shouting. She found them girls about her age, and soon made their acquaintance, joining in the fun. As they were staying at the hotel, they proved to be pleasant playmates for her.

"We will show you all the nice places to play. We take our dollies, and go down to the river bank, and play under the bridge, where it is shady."

"Oh! mamma, you *must* unpack my doll just as soon as you can, for we are going to play house, down by the river."

"I am afraid to have you go there without some one to look after you, as I don't know what danger there might be in a strange place."

"Well, have Nellie take Pearl in her carriage and go with us."

So they started with their doll-children, who looked rather pale, as if they needed an airing. There was a long bridge, crossing the river to the other side. The children found a nice shady place near it, where large rocks could serve as seats and tables in this play-house.

Little Pearl was delighted with the rippling

water and the smooth stones, which the children gathered for her. She would toss them about, talking and cooing in baby fashion. It was a pretty sight to see the children thus occupied, little Pearl in the midst, the breeze blowing her hair about, and the sunlight making every thing look so bright and gay.

So thought Mrs. Grey and the other ladies, who, tired of keeping quiet, had come down to see if the little ones were safe. They also liked the spot so much it was not until the gong sounded for dinner that they wanted to go to the house.

"How glad I am we came, dear mamma, it is so much nicer than the city in a hot day!"

"Do n't you miss the Common and playing with your girls, as you call them?"

"Oh! yes, I love the dear old Common; still we can play there any time, but can only be in the real country a little while."

"You are right, my dear; enjoy all you can, wherever you may be; *that* is the true secret of happiness."

So every day they found some pleasant spot in which to pass the leisure hours away. One of the greatest pleasures was the drives, which they took about the country in large mountain wagons. The merry company would soon fill these vehicles, going over the roads at a lively pace, for the spirited horses seemed to take delight in seeing how many miles they could travel. It was such fun to trot up and down the long hills, passing the farm-houses, the big barns filled with fragrant hay, fields of golden grain waving in the breeze, and orchards with the ripening fruit—pictures of comfort. Sometimes the whole family could be seen at the windows, gazing upon the merry company of "city folks" as they drove past.

"Happy country life," said one.

"Yes, happy indeed, the very care of gathering in the fruits seems easy in contrast to our city duties," added another.

"I am afraid we would sigh for our cosy homes in the bleak winter time."

"Perhaps, but it is so lovely now."

On one of these drives, they entered a broad, shady road. There were two wagons, each having four seats, and every one was occupied. The driver halted under a beautiful row of elm trees, which was on one side of the road, opposite a large white house. An American flag was floating in the breeze near it.

"Why are we stopping here?"

"Whose house is that on the other side?"

"A fine place, and what lovely great. trees about it!"

"This is the Daniel Webster house, where he lived many years."

At that moment a tall gray-haired gentleman came to the door. He lifted his hat to the company, invited them to alight and enter the house. Before doing this Mr. Grey began to sing the "Star-spangled Banner," in which all joined, even the dignified colonel who was waiting to escort his visitors in. It was an outburst of patriotic feeling, love for their own beautiful land, and admiration for the memory of their brilliant countryman, filling their hearts. They were shown into the cool parlor, modern in every way.

The colonel, who owned the estate, told them that the original house was the L they had seen. He had built the present residence, but kept the old part in memory of the great man. He then took them into the old study, or library. It was a small, low-studded room, plainly furnished. A large, old-fashioned, hair-cloth sofa, with high back, a desk at which Webster wrote, and a large arm-chair near it, a book-case full of well-worn volumes, a few odd chairs, and an oil-cloth covering on the floor completed the furnishings of this room.

Here it was that this great scholar penned the thoughts which were received by the world with applause. The company all took turns sitting in the old chair and on the sofa, handling the books with care, which had been his helpers.

It was indeed a great privilege to be able to *touch* the every-day belongings of such a man.

Frances was the youngest of the party, and she also had her turn, that she might in after days think of this experience.

Daniel Webster was one of the greatest men of his day; when his voice was heard among his countrymen it was a power, swaying all by its eloquence. Even the boys and girls of to-day may reverence the memory of this writer and orator, and study to improve their talents as he did.

There were other rooms in this original part which had been daily used by him, but this old study was the center, in which his noble thoughts and aims had taken life for the good of his country.

They at last bade good-bye to the hospitable colonel, and departed, much pleased with this visit to an old landmark.

There was a little town some miles away, nestled in among the hills. In sight was old Mount Kearsarge, its hoary top rising into the very clouds. It was a quiet village, but a church spire showed that the people who lived there remembered the Father in Heaven.

On Sundays the fathers and mothers, with the little children, went there to hear the good minister, who told them how to live pure lives, of benefit to those about them.

Mr. Grey knew this preacher and his wife, so a plan was made to give them a surprise call, carry their own lunch, and spend part of the day in their home.

A party of twenty started bright and early, for it was a long ride. It was just refreshing to breathe in the pure mountain breeze, and how lovely the shadows looked as they came and went on the mountains! Frances liked to watch for the little brooks and see the water rush down over the rocks, as a real waterfall came in view. Then the wild flowers were so gorgeous,—the queen of the meadow, the yellow daisies, and the golden-rod, which was just coming out.

She wanted to stop and gather them all. When they rested the horses, after a hard pull up the long hills, under the shade of the trees, she would run into the nearest field, and come back with her hands full of these treasures. How cool it looked in the shady woods!

"Oh! mamma, how lovely! If it was always so we should want to stay forever."

Once in a while a gray squirrel would dart across the road, or a little chipmunk run along the stone wall. Then they would pass houses dark with age, the roofs sloping to the ground, the gardens filled with hollyhocks, sun-flowers, and bachelor-buttons. They stopped at one of these houses, to ask for a drink of water from the old well, which stood near the road. A number of children were playing about, and one sturdy lad put the bucket at-tached to the well-sweep into the well, drew it up dripping from the sparkling water.

Frances, looking down into the opening, could see in the water below, her face dis-tinctly, shining out from the depths into which she looked. The mother of the children came out with a pan full of doughnuts, which the strangers much enjoyed. The bracing air had made them hungry early in the day.

After thanking the family for their kindness, they were once more on their way, feeling much refreshed. A good many long hills were still before them, but the hardy horses, trained to the work, soon lessened the distance.

One more steep ascent, and the village they sought was reached. A quiet place, with a number of pretty white cottages, one store, a school-house, and a church, clustered about the village green, on which in a prominent place was the town-pump, keeping guard over all.

Quite a commotion was made by the clatter of the horses' feet, and the rumble of the wagons as they came into the village. Many eyes were eagerly watching, as they drew up in front of the minister's house. The good wife quickly opened the door, with a warm welcome for the visitors. They had hardly reached the ground before her husband came to see the meaning of all this noise in the usually quiet street. At last he began to think that they had come to see him, and a cordial greeting was given.

"Welcome to our quiet home, young and old," he said.

"We have come a quite a distance to give you a call," said Mr. Grey.

" But we feel repaid already, it was such a fine ride," said his wife.

"As the old saying is, We have come to see the folks and get some peaches."

"We will give you the best our village affords, but I am afraid not many peaches," said the minister.

He very soon knew that it was not for him to provide the feast, for the table was loaded shortly with all kinds of goodies, which they had brought with them. Frances made a large bouquet for the center of the table, of the wild flowers which she had picked. They were lovely and "just like the *real* country," she said. It was a day full of joy and pleasure, long remembered by them.

After dinner the clouds had darkened, and a thunder-shower threatened, which came in a downfall of rain. It just poured for some hours, but at last the sun shone out, and the blue sky appeared. Then a start must be made, or darkness would overtake them. So the wagons were again filled, and the echo of the good-byes was heard among the hills. As they rode along, the scene before them was just wonderful. Even the children felt the beauty in their hearts. Frances sat very still, with her hand in mamma's.

"Oh! I wish I never could forget this lovely picture."

"All we can do is to take away with us all of the glory we can."

They could see peak upon peak, covered by a soft haze, melting away in the distance; green valleys, with the broad river Pemigewasset flowing through; great trees waving their branches in the evening breeze; the sky so blue, with banks of white clouds, lit up by the rosy gleams of the setting sun, which was just going down behind Mount Kearsarge. It was indeed glorious, and the company rode home almost in silence, for it would not seem right to break the charm of the hour.

So the time slipped rapidly by, and the happy company must leave these pleasant scenes, for duty called. Frances could not find time to write letters every day as she had promised, but she wrote to Mary after this lovely ride:—

FRANKLIN, *Aug. 2d.*

" *Dearest Mary:*

" I write this letter so you may know that I have not forgotten you *entirely.* I am having such a gorgeous time that I don't write much. There are some nice children here, but they are not just like our girls.

We all go to ride every day, in big wagons, and

the other day went to see the Daniel Webster house. We saw the very chair, desk, and sofa which he used every day. I sat down at the desk, and wrote my name with the very pen he had used.

" Only think of it !

" Papa said that it was a great honor to even touch these things.

"The colonel, who owns this house was a dear old man like our friend of the Hancock House, who gives us the lilacs. We gave him three cheers before we rode away. Hugh — the rogue — ought to have been here to help us shout.

"One morning we had breakfast at six o'clock, and went for a long drive. I can't begin to tell you what fun it was. When the hills were very long, we children would jump out and walk up. We had a drink from an old well. A boy drew it up for us, and we drank it out of a tin dipper. He was very polite, even if he wore a ragged hat and was barefoot. The well was very deep, but I could see my face in it ; yes, and my auburn locks.

"We gave a surprise call to a minister and his wife. We carried our dinner, every thing good, I tell you. We had so much that we could not posibly eat it all, so left it. The minister said it was a gift call. A terrible thunder shower came up. I was very frightened for a little while, but it was so lovely after it was over ! All we could do was to just look, as we rode home ; it was too fine to even speak a word. I can write a composition about the mountains, sky, and clouds, if I can think of words good enough to describe what we saw.

" Vacation will soon be over in a few weeks, then for school again. We are going to auntie's on our way home, to see what Ed. has been doing all this time.

"I hope you are having just as good a time at the seashore as we are in the country.

"Write soon and tell me all *your* news.

"With best love and a dozen kisses,

"Yours ever loving,

"FRANCES G——.

"P. S. I feel just as bad as ever about the diploma. I do n't like to think of it.

"F. S. G."

The day came when farewell must be said to the mountains and all the places where so many pleasant hours had been spent. So with thanks to their kind host and family, they were again on the way.

The Greys arrived in the pleasant country town where auntie lived, and were driven to the farm. As they went up into the door-yard, auntie came out from the house, giving them a warm welcome. Just then a boy came around the corner of the barn. He wore a ragged straw hat, the crown being almost gone, so that his bright hair could be seen, he was barefooted, his clothes were in the same state as his hat, his face and hands were both brown and black, but his eyes looked bright and full of roguery as he saw the newcomers. Mamma looked rather startled as she said, "Why! *that* boy can't be my Ed.!"

" I think he must have been some relation to him, once on a time," replied papa.

"Oh! it is Ed., mamma, but what a ragamuffin!"

"That is my hired boy and he has been digging potatoes for dinner," said auntie.

Meanwhile he had come out in full view, but looked rather sheepish, as he began to think how funny he must look to them. It did n't make any difference, however, for mamma hugged him, dirty and ragged as he was.

"You are a regular country boy now."

"Yes, and it 's real jolly fun, but I hurt my feet sometimes on the stones in the pastures."

They were glad to find him so rugged and well, for he was rather a delicate boy at home. Now Frances must be shown all his haunts, see where the woodchucks lived, go berrying, drive the cow to pasture in the morning and home at night, feed the hens and chickens, and hunt for eggs.

The greatest treat of all was to go with auntie "downtown" to sell the berries, and have her buy "peppermints," she said, to eat on the way, as they jogged homeward.

The vacation was nearly over, and school days were again at hand.

"I wish I could stay here all winter," said Ed.

"Then you would like to be a real farmer? I think you hardly know all that means."

"Auntie, do you want to keep my boy?" said papa, laughing.

"Yes, if he would like to stay."

Ed., however, thought he would go home, when he saw the trunks being packed. He liked his school and playmates, but the country had many charms for both the children. Auntie drove them to the station, and as the cars were leaving they saw her wiping her eyes, as they went out of sight. She dearly loved the children, and missed them very much when they went away.

As soon as possible after Frances had arrived she went to Mary's house to inquire about her. The door was opened by Mary herself, who hugged her "within an inch of her life," she said. Then they went the rounds, and found Kitty and Annie Bell ready to welcome them.

How the tongues flew, and "Oh! girls"; "Say, what do you think?" and "Gorgeous time!" were heard at intervals, as they described their vacation.

School was to begin on Monday, and at that time all the familiar faces were seen. These friends were all promoted to a higher class, and had a new teacher. Now harder studies were to be met. They had been well prepared by the last year's work, so it would be all the easier to go forward in their duties.

The fair was now the great interest outside of school. Every spare moment was given by the girls in preparing for this event. Each one invited her friends to make some pretty and useful article for this object. They were to have the fair in Mary's house, and were thinking up all sorts of plans to make every thing attractive. Mary's sister Sarah had been married during the summer. She and her husband were at home, and felt much interested in this plan.

" Mr. Edward," as the young folks called him, was a great friend, and any important question to be settled was always left to him. He was very kind and seemed as young as any of them.

Of course the Sewing-Circle was a source of profit, as Aunt Fannie and Sister Sarah showed them how to make many pretty things. Frances had not forgotten her plan of gathering ferns, mosses, and leaves, to arrange in different shapes. She bought some stiff cardboard, cut it into various forms similar to an artist's palette, a cross and also as a wreath. Then she arranged the ferns and leaves upon these shapes, keeping them in place by gum-arabic.

They were just lovely! The pictures where she used the mosses with the ferns, placing little acorn cups in the moss, were pretty and looked very natural, making one think of the woods. She also made round silk balls of different colors, filled with perfume, and placed them, held by gum-arabic, in the acorn cups; then putting a number of these together by wire, and tying them with ribbon, a sweet-scented bouquet was the result.

Thus by using a little thought, so many pretty things can be made out of the simplest materials.

At one of the afternoon meetings, they were busily talking over the best plans for the fair, when Mr. Edward opened the door, saying, " May *I* come in ? "

" Yes, indeed! We want to see you about lots of things."

He sat down in the midst, and at once they plied him with questions.

" We must have ice-cream and cake to sell, do you think we can ? "

"Where can we have it served?"

"I should think the small study would do nicely; two of the girls can be waiters, and dress up in white aprons and caps."

"I can help dish it out," said Hugh.

"Let Kitty and Etta be the waiter girls for the first day, then have two others the next."

"We are willing."

"Now you must hold this fair before Christmas, so that people can then buy their presents."

"Mr. Edward, you must trim the tables for us and put up flags in the hall. Don't you think it will look pretty?"

"Yes, I like the idea very much, and perhaps we can arrange colored lanterns, to make the entrance look bright in the evening."

"Oh! Mr. Edward, you are a jewel!"

"We are so glad you are here to help us!"

They wished him to be the manager, and tell each one just what to do at the time of the fair. So he made out a list of their duties, and they all knew just what was expected.

The appointed day was near at hand, and the workers were hurrying to get all in order. Frances had received a great many articles in answer to her requests, and was highly delighted with the box full of pretty things; knit worsted balls, pin-cushions, needle-books, little socks and sacks for dolls, and a baby doll, which was dressed like a "real baby," she said. These, with what she had made herself, formed a nice collection, but, best of all, her grandpa had made a number of rulers from wood of the Old Elm Tree on the Common. A large branch had blown off, and he had obtained a portion of it. They were very nice as keepsakes of the ancient tree.

The evening before was spent in fixing the tables and trimming the pictures with Christmas wreaths. These, with red, white, and blue bunting and flags, made the rooms and hall look bright and gay. Japanese lanterns were hung at the entrance. A friend of Annie Bell's had promised her some cut flowers, and she was to make button-hole bouquets for the young gentlemen to buy.

"Perhaps Charlie Howard may buy one, if you have them to sell," said Kitty.

"Well, I guess *some one* will buy a dozen ice-creams if you have them to sell," answered Annie.

"I hope the people will like the things so well that we shall not have one left," said Mary.

The fair was to open in the afternoon at two o'clock. From that time until ten o'clock the friends of the children were constantly coming. Every thing looked so tasteful, and the articles for sale were so pretty and useful, that the girls were kept busy in disposing of them. Annie Bell had a small table by herself, where the bouquets could be bought. She soon sold all that were made, and arranged more as they were wanted. Charlie Howard was one of the ushers, so of course he bought one for himself, and then gave another to Annie from her own use, "if she would accept it."

"Thank you very much," she said with a beaming smile, and placed it at her throat for safe keeping.

As he turned away Kitty came up to the table, saying slyly, "What did I tell you, I knew a certain person would buy your flowers."

"Yes," said Annie with a blush, "he is very kind and polite, see he gave me this one!"

"Oh! how nice, I wish some one would think of me," laughed Kitty.

"Well, my dear child, it shall be as you wish," said Mr. Edward as he put a lovely bunch in her hand. "I must treat you all alike," he said, and forthwith the bouquets Annie then had on

her table were distributed to the girls. Her
money-box was getting quite full already.

The little study had been prettily trimmed
and it was a pleasant place in which to rest and
eat ice-cream. Etta and Kitty were very nice
waiter girls, and they quite enjoyed their duties.
The dainty dishes, the bright silver, the nice
cake, and the pretty girls, with bright eyes and
smiling faces. who were to serve the refresh-
ments, made it an attractive corner. On one
end of the large table home-made candy was
to be found, it was very nice and sold rapidly
among the children.

The boys all wanted a ruler made from the
"Old Elm," and the girls bought the dolls' sacks
and socks. The older people were much pleased with the fern pictures, and they sold quickly. The rooms looked even prettier in the
evening, after the gas was lit; the bright flags
and Japanese lanterns blending with the evergreen; a crackling log-fire made it seem home-
like and warm, after being out in the winter air,
for it was real biting cold Christmas weather.

So all went off very pleasantly as the merry
voices and gay laughter of the visitors proved
their enjoyment.

The plan for the second day was somewhat different. The time to open the fair was to be six o'clock. As only a few things were left to be sold, they were to have games in the evening for an hour or two. The remaining articles were to be bid off at "auction," and Mr. Edward was the auctioneer. It was great fun, and the boys always managed to bid the highest.

Frances' music-teacher was to play the piano for them.

A merry time they had, listening to " Virginia Reel," " Portland Fancy," and the " Polka Redowa."

At last the happy evening was at an end, and the fair for which these young folks had worked so hard was over. It had been a great success in every way, and the sum of money which had been obtained was nearly fifty dollars. A part of this money was to be given to one of the city missions, and the rest was to be kept for use, to help some poor family whenever it should be needed. It was really quite a hard thing for these friends to carry out this plan of a fair; but they were able to do so, as their kind parents and friends were so willing to help them in the good work. A very little thing will often be the starting point of a great good. As

Mary said, "If it had n't been for Bridget Nolan coming to beg, and looking so ragged, we never should have wanted to make clothes for poor children."

Aunt Fannie said, "that some good would come of it, even after she wore the old rags again, and did n't go to school."

The children were to go with Mr. Edward to visit the mission and present the gift at that time. It is well for young people to have an interest in those about them, and lend a helping hand early in life. Thus by being thoughtful of the comfort of others, they can be missionaries at home and abroad, every day of their lives.

During this time, Frances had kept up her practice in music, and was doing very nicely. She was faithful and always went to Rosa's house at the appointed hour. She would sometimes say, "How I wish I had a piano of my own! Then I could play just when I felt like it."

"Perhaps your wish may be realized some day, if you still continue to improve," said papa.

"I am afraid it will be a long time if we wait to get rich."

Papa laughed, but did not continue the conversation.

At the end of the second quarter of lessons Rosa Lane invited Mr. and Mrs. Grey to hear Frances play, that they might judge of her progress. She could now play a number of simple pieces, besides the exercises. They were very much pleased and thought she had made good use of her time.

"Oh! if I only could have a piano at home, I might practise ever so much more."

Mrs. Grey said, "Frances has always some great want, which after a while seems to be satisfied."

"It may be so now," said Rosa.

"It is such a big want that I am sure I never can have one; at least, for ever so long a time."

A few weeks after this, Frances came in from afternoon school, went upstairs into Mrs. Grey's room, to say that she was going to practise her music-lesson.

Mamma said, "I wish you would step into the parlor before you go and bring me the book with the blue cover, which you will find on the centre table."

Frances did n't really want to stop, but she

ran to do the errand. She entered the parlor, which was somewhat dark; she struck her hand very hard against something, that she did not know was so near the door. She stopped to look at the object, and found to her surprise a nice piano standing in the corner, looking as if it had always been in that same place.

"Mamma, come down here, just as quickly as you can," she cried, running to the foot of the stairs.

"What is it, my dear?"

"You just come in the parlor, and tell me *how* this piano came here."

Mamma laughed, saying, "I think some strong men must have brought it in, for it is very heavy."

"Is it for me?"

"Yes, my dear child," said papa's voice, as he came into the room, followed by Ed., who wanted to see how Frances would like being surprised this time. "We thought you were so faithful to your music, and had made such good progress, that you deserved to be rewarded."

"Oh! darling papa, how good you are to me! Now I can play ever so much."

"We hope you will enjoy it and go on improving."

"This almost makes up for not getting the diploma."

"Now, sis, play us a tune," said Ed. He lighted the gas as he spoke, and she sat down, to play the very best she could.

" That 's fine ; you can give a concert some day."

She must go to tell Rosa why she did n't come to her house, and also to get her music to practise at home.

"I have the loveliest piano of my own; you must come and play for us, Rosa."

" I shall be very happy to do so. I knew you were going to have it."

"Oh! why did n't you tell me about it?"

" I thought you would like to be surprised."

"Well, I do, and I feel so happy I could dance for joy."

"You must try all the more to improve, and I think you will make a nice player."

Frances had never forgotten the bitter trial she had in losing the diploma, but now it seemed as if this quite made up for her grief at that time.

So it often is in life; when we have a trouble a joy will come, which will make all seem bright to us. The girls were just as delighted as

Frances was, and duly praised the piano. She had a little party one evening, that they all might try its tone. Mary played for them to sing, and a pleasant hour was spent, christening the new piano.

THE OLD SOUTH CHURCH.

VIII.

THE BLACK CAT.

FROM day to day new thoughts, feelings, and ambitions find a place even in the minds of children. When they wake in the morning some new idea will spring up which they are eager to take in hand. So it was with these young folks; they were always thinking of some new thing, which with the old duties kept them busy. School was the first on the list, and other pleasures followed.

Now the plan in prospect was the bringing out of a dialogue called "The Black Cat," which showed the evils of slavery. About this time rumors of war were heard in this country, the events of which the children of to-day are now studying. These young folks lived in the very days of the conflict, and remember the stirring times even in quiet Boston.

Perhaps they could hardly realize the hardship and peril to those who were called upon to take part in this struggle. Their lives flowed on quietly, without much trouble or change.

They heard the older people talking of this battle and that general, and knew that many brave
men had gone from their homes to help save
their country. They all had some near friend
or relative who was a soldier. Frances knew
how auntie cried every day, when she spoke of
her son who was gone. She always felt sorry
for her, and wished the war was over, that he
might come home. In every family either a
son, brother, uncle or cousin was missing from
the circle. Frances often saw her papa look
very sober as he read the morning paper, saying, " A terrible battle at Ball's Bluff," or later
on at " Gettysburg, hundreds of our boys lost!"

"Oh! the cruel war which must sacrifice so
many brave men," sighed Mrs. Grey.

Frances or her friends in their happy homes,
shielded from all harm, could not know the
danger so distant from them. They often
went, however, into the busy streets, to watch
the regiments from all parts of New England,
which were passing through the city on their
way to Washington. The men looked so brave
and handsome in their military dress, as they
marched along, keeping time to the music! It
seemed hardly possible that only a few of the
many would return to their homes.

"Brave boys, may the Good Father watch over them," Mr. Grey would say as he watched these sturdy men.

Many of his own Sunday-school boys had come to him for a last good-bye.

"God bless you, sir! You have been a kind friend to us."

He often received letters from them, telling him of their welfare. The children learned to sing, "John Brown," "Marching through Georgia," and "Tenting To-night on the Old Camp Ground."

So the days, weeks, and months flew by, and home-life went on the usual way, although the country was in peril. The girls and boys were asked to take the parts in this dialogue, which was to be given in a hall, in aid of a children's hospital, — Frances as North; Annie, South; Etta, Mexico; Kitty, France; Hugh, Slavery; Charlie Howard, England; and Mary, the Goddess of Liberty. It was quite an exciting dialogue, with a number of fine tableaux and patriotic songs introduced and very nicely arranged.

The young folks worked hard for several weeks to get their parts learned perfectly, and many rehearsals were necessary to blend the whole together.   They entered into the spirit of it, and were busy preparing their costumes or dresses for the evening.

The time came, and the hall was packed with a large audience.   The performers were flying around in the dressing-rooms, to get ready in season, and sashes, ribbons, flags, pins, needles, and flowers were floating everywhere.   At last the finishing touches were made by the ladies in charge; but none too soon, for the clock said half-past seven, and the curtain rose at that time.

The bell rang.   Frances, as North, appeared in a blue dress, with white drapery and red ribbons, carrying an American flag in her hand; Annie, as South, was dressed in grey, the southern color.   A spirited dialogue was given by them, and both sides of the question brought forward.

Then Mexico, France, and England appeared in turn, and Slavery showed the wrong done to the colored race; Mary, as Goddess of Liberty, came in; she looked very lovely in her pure white dress, with the flag wrapped in folds about her, wearing a crown on her golden curls.   She stepped upon a platform, and then addressed those about her in stirring words of love for their country, of brotherly affection, and mercy for the down-trodden race, who were held in bondage. As she finished, the ever-new " Star-spangled Banner," was taken up by the young people, and at the last a rosy light shed upon all made the scene really beautiful. Loyalty to their country shone in the faces of these young people, and their eyes sparkled with the spirit of courage.

This was the end, a hearty applause broke forth, which was fairly earned, for they had all done splendidly. After other appropriate songs a nice treat was given, which, with the praise they received, amply repaid them for the hard work done.

Care must be taken of the little ones left at home, who were suffering while the work of sending comforts to the soldiers in the camps and hospitals was still going on.

A gentleman friend of the Lees was to journey South, to help care for the wounded soldiers, and to aid them in any way he could. He was to take with him articles of use, as well as nourishing food for the poor sick men, and all were to be remembered who were in the service of the country. The girls now busied themselves in making needle books and pin balls, made of cardboard covered with silk or bright woolen. They each sent a testament with the name of the giver in it. How many of these little gifts were treasured by "the boys in blue," and alas! carried to their last resting-place, as they were folded in their army blankets for the final sleep.

Frances was much surprised to receive a letter, dated from a southern city and written in a manly hand, thanking her for the testament which had been given to the writer. He was a soldier from New York state, and was a farmer's son, but had left the fields to carry a musket in defense of the rights of his country.

When a boy he had always been to Sunday school; he had lost the bible which his mother had placed in his hand, on his departure for the war, in a battle where all belongings were left behind in order to save his life. He felt very grateful for this gift from the little Boston girl.

"How funny, mamma, that a New York boy should receive a remembrance from a Massachusetts girl!"

"Strange things often happen, and we are brought very close together in this time of doubt and uncertainty."

So the time rolled on, and it was not only weeks and months, but years—one, two, three— and still the struggle went on, until four had nearly passed. These girls and their friends kept pace with the march of time, and were now nearing that boundary between childhood and girlhood. In a few years, hardly before they could realize the change, they would be grown up, ready to take their place in the world. Every year added some new grace and improvement, an ambition to excel in either music, painting, or the various accomplishments of the needle; also to cultivate a taste for the beautiful, wherever it might be found, and then be able to put in words, as well as on the canvas, the life going on around them.

They were now in the master's class, studying as hard as ever to prepare themselves for a higher school, as well as to graduate with honor. The promise of their childhood had been a true one, and they were a fine group of girls,—smart and bright, eager to take hold of life in earnest.

Frances had made good use of the privilege of having a piano, and was really becoming a fine player. Mary and herself spent many pleasant hours in practising duets, which were a source of delight to their friends.   Little Pearl was a great favorite and always received a warm welcome.   She dearly loved music, and often her little fingers would make the piano speak.

" I guess Pearl is a born musician," her friends would say.

One day, as they were sitting in the pleasant old play-room at Mary's, busily engaged in sewing,—for their interest in the Circle still was fresh, and good clothes were always in demand,— Mary said, " I say, girls, have you thought what kind of dresses we are to wear for graduation?   I want something fine."

" Well, I know mamma does not wish me to have a thin muslin, and I do n't like a woolen dress for such a time," said Frances.

" I think we ought to have them all different, but I want mine 'stunning,' as the boys say," said Kitty.

"Oh! fie, girls, talking about your dresses when you ought to be thinking of your compositions," said Hugh, as he came into the room, followed by Charlie Howard and Frank Bliss, "The Inseparables," as the girls called them.

The boys had grown to be tall lads, but were as full of mischief as ever.

"Well, so you must look just as pretty as ever you can," laughed Hugh.

"I have my composition written, ready to copy, and Mr. Babcock is to decide which ones are to be read at the graduation," said Frances.

"Yes, and we are to read that poem called 'The Young Gray Head.' It is a beautiful thing, but quite long, so it will be divided into parts."

"I say, girls, there is to be a declamation at the Latin School on Saturday, and you must go, for I am to speak 'Whittier's Slave Ship,'" said Charlie Howard.

"That will be fine, and we must all go," said Mary.

"Papa said that he thought the war was almost over, and Richmond, the capital of the Confederate States, must soon be ours," said Frances.

"Yes, hurrah for General Grant!"

"Three cheers for the Union army!" shouted the boys.

"Gracious, what a noise!"

"Never mind, if we only save the North and free the slaves!"

"Papa said that our dear President Lincoln had done a great deed in freeing them, and that his fame would live as long as the world stood," said Frances.

"I wish I could have been a soldier. It must be glorious to fight for one's country," said Hugh.

"Yes, my dear boy, it is a noble thing to be courageous, but you can help your country by living a true and honest life, and lending a helping hand to those about you, even if you can not go to the war and be a real soldier," said Aunt Fannie.

So they talked, these young people who were to be the men and women, their hearts full of zeal and patriotic feeling, but still hardly knowing the peril through which their own homes had passed, now that the end was near which should restore peace to the land. Their home comforts had never ceased; they had been watched over by loving friends, while the brave soldiers were at the front defending these homes.

One morning Mr. Grey waved nis paper in the air, saying, "Richmond is ours! General Lee has surrendered."

The glad cry was taken up all over the country, where loyalty to the Stars and Stripes still remained, for now the long and cruel war was nearly over. But alas ! the joy of victory was soon dimmed by a great sadness. It seemed but a day when the news flashed over the world that President Lincoln was shot by the hand of an enemy and could live but a few days. Frances opened the door for her papa, who came hurriedly in, looking very pale.

" The good man has gone to his reward," he said, and his eyes were full of tears, for he felt that the noble man was like a brother to him, and a benefactor to his country.

Every loyal man, woman, and child bowed their heads in mourning for their loved president. It seemed like magic, after the news was received, how quickly the city of Boston, was draped in black. Forgotten were business, school, and household cares. The streets were filled with people, who left all behind to be together in this time of sorrow, to pray for the family of the dead hero, and ask God to still lead them in the right way. The houses, public buildings, and stores were soon draped in black, the merchants taking the goods from their counters to do this, and every person wore a badge of mourning, even the little ones having a rosette made of black ribbon upon them. But no outward sign could fully express the sorrow of the nation.   Frances and her friends went with Mr. Grey to walk about. Everywhere the city was crowded with people, and the Common seemed to be the meeting-place for all to assemble, to talk over this sudden blow.

A day never to be forgotten, the air soft and spring-like, the sun shining brightly, the sky so blue, but still a black cloud was there, so dark that it made all seem like night.

In after life they often thought of this day, when they walked on the Common under the beautiful trees, wearing an emblem of sorrow for the "Martyr President."   They were living in stirring times, and great questions to be settled and opportunities to be taken up were before these young spirits, but the influence of this noble life was ever felt by them in the days of manhood and womanhood.

Important events happen; still the little things of life make a great part of living. School must go on, and every-day duties have their place.   Mary's house was still a favorite resort, and many pleasant hours were spent, talking over their plans.   They had happened in, one day, and were eagerly talking of the events which were to take place.

"Well, Frances, so your composition has been chosen," said Etta.

"I knew it would be so, for you are splendid in that line," said Annie Bell.

"I can write easily, but I am still so stupid in arithmetic it makes my rank in the class lower than it should be," replied Frances.

"Mary, you will lead the class, for your average is the very highest," said Kitty.

"We all keep so near together, no one can boast very much," answered Mary.

It was so indeed, and the master was proud of his leading girls, as well as of the whole class.

Etta said, "I dread the Normal-school examination; perhaps it will not be any harder than our own, which we have had."

"It will seem so different, to have all strangers about us. I know my ideas will all fly away, when I get to the spelling. I shall put *e* before *i*, and make all kinds of silly mistakes," said Annie.

"I know I shall get bank discount mixed up with square root, and sha'n't know a fraction when I see it," laughed Frances.

"Oh! pshaw, girls, how you talk! I know you will do well if you try," answered Mary.

"We shall look at your shining countenance and gain courage," replied Kitty.

"Was n't the declamation at the Latin School splendid?"

"Yes, and Charlie Howard did finely."

"I think all the speakers were good and did their very best. Charlie Howard is fitting for college, and I want Hugh to enter the Latin School, but he wishes to be a business man, so father thinks he will have him study for that purpose, probably at the High School," said Mary.

"Mary, what shall you do after you are grown up?"

"I should like to be a teacher, for I love study so much that I never wish to put it aside."

"Well, I like to compose so much that I shall *try* to be a writer, even if I do n't succeed," said Frances.

"Heigho! I have not thought so far ahead as that. Don't be serious, but come for a stroll and see what pretty ribbons we can find, for I must decide about the color for my dress," said Kitty.

"Heavenly blue, dear, to match your eyes," laughed Etta.

"Rose pink for you, then, to match your cheeks," replied the light-hearted girl, as she danced around the room, humming a gay polka.

So they started out for a walk on the dear old Common, and visited some of the stores in search of "the prettiest thing out." Happy youth, pleased with any new fancy or fashion! It is well, for the cares of life come all too soon. Still the young people, the girls as well as the boys, should be taught that they have an object or study in life, and that their influence will be felt in the world.

The Graduation Day was near at hand, and all were in a flutter to have every thing a success. The hall was decorated with bunting, and the platform covered with pot-plants, the master's desk being ornamented with lovely bouquets.

The programme was a varied one, and very interesting to the audience. The singing, the Class Poem, the original composition — "The Fine Arts" — by Frances Grey, and the Valedictory by Mary Swan, were all gems; the poem, "The Young Gray Head," was listened to with great interest. It was read by five of the class, and the sad story was well brought out by them.

A lovely group of girls, as they stood together for this exercise: Mary, her golden curls tied back with white ribbon, her pretty dress, and her face full of intelligence, made a lovely picture; Frances, slight and fair, in appearance so thoughtful; Kitty, tall and slender, with a look of mischief in her blue eyes; Etta, her cheeks red with excitement, and their classmate, Jennie Brown, a fine-looking girl, formed a circle of which their teacher might well be proud,—all unconscious of their loveliness, thinking only of the duty before them, which must be well done. Boston has been and may well be proud of her school graduates. They do honor to their training, all over the world.

Then the class received diplomas of graduation. The little roll of paper, tied with blue ribbon, was a token of a course of study ended, which prepared them to enter fields of higher knowledge. At the close of these exercises, and after the friends had gone, the girls gathered about their loved master, also the good assistant, to say good-bye and to listen to his words of encouragement.

"Now, girls, do your very best at the examination; you are all capable of good work. I feel proud of my girls to-day." So with his words sounding in their ears they went forth to victory.

The test was a hard one, and the girls were doubtful of the result.

"I do feel so nervous about it, for I am afraid I have not done well, and there are two whole days to pass, before we know the decision," said Frances.

"Possess your soul in patience," said Ed. "I have been through the same thing myself."

"You did the best you could, so now you must try to be contented," said mamma.

"Well, I felt 'so flustrated,' as Kitty said, with all those strange teachers looking at us, that I couldn't do half so well as in the dear old school-room."

The two days passed, and the girls went to hear the verdict. It would be known in either one of the words, "admitted" or "rejected." They were each to go into a room alone to hear the decision. Mary Swan had been called. Frances was trembling with anxiety, dreading, yet wishing, to know her success. She could hardly walk, as she rose in answer to the call of her name, but as the welcome word "admitted" was spoken, she could hardly realize that it was true. Then Kitty, followed by Etta, soon appeared, all with smiling faces.

"Glory! I 've passed," cried Kitty.

"So have I," was repeated by the voices.

"I know I looked pale, for I felt so when I went into that room," said Frances.

"I knew Mary would be all right."

"Well, I think it was a very hard examination."

"We can rest now in our minds, and have a good time at the Fourth of July Festival," said Etta.

"It is too bad Annie will not be with us next year; her mother is so ill that she must live South, and Annie is to go to boarding-school."

"I do hope aunt will allow me to take the whole course, now I have passed, but she thinks I ought to stay at home and help her. At any rate I have the satisfaction of knowing I was admitted," said Etta.

"Oh! I guess your aunt will give you one year more for school," replied Mary.

"We shall feel lonesome to miss any of the girls," replied Frances.

"There, don't worry, girls, but think of the fun we shall have at the festival," chimed in Kitty.

It would seem that pleasure and good times formed a large share of the lives of these girls. They were indeed privileged to have their young days full of happiness, with so many good times that the years were marked with pleasure as well as profit. This particular celebration was always remembered by them with delight, and a hearty laugh indulged in when they talked over the day.

The young people assembled in Bumstead Hall, which is in Music Hall building, in due season. They were to sing patriotic songs in accord with the other exercises; the Declaration of Independence was to be read, and speeches made by prominent men of the city. They were almost ready to go into the hall above, when a gentleman in charge called for order, as he wished to say a few words.

"My young friends, we have just become aware that the collation, which is always given to our singers, has not been ordered for to-day, which we much regret. We would like to have you choose from two plans. Will you have fifty cents apiece, or come here to-morrow and have a collation?"

The boys shouted, "Fifty cents, sir!"

The girls said, "Oh! let us have the collation!"

The gentleman laughed, and after talking for a few moments, the good man came forward and said, "Well, young folks, we have decided to give you all fifty cents to-day, and then have a collation to-morrow.   So both the boys and girls will be pleased."

Such a shout as was given, and the clapping of hands was almost deafening.   At last order was restored, and they filed into Music Hall, which was again decorated with flags and bunting.   Their delight was shown by the spirited manner in which they gave the songs of Freedom.

The next day found them all there, ready to enjoy the good time which had been promised them.

"Dear old Music Hall, what fine times we have enjoyed within its walls!" said Frances.

Indeed it was so, and this day was just as enjoyable.   They enjoyed the strains of the merry music, such as the Germania band knew how to give; then a bountiful collation of ice-cream, cake, and other goodies was provided.

As the girls were standing in a group, Frances suddenly said, "Why! I declare, there is Fred Green over by that door; and he is looking this way; he must have seen me."

"Do you mean the one with two other gentlemen standing near him?"

"Yes, they must be some of his friends."

At that moment Frances received a polite bow from the young man, and he smilingly came forward to greet her.

"I did not think of seeing you here, Miss Frances," he said, "but I am very glad to meet you"; and Frances repaid the compliment by presenting her friends.

"Allow me to introduce my friends. We have just come from the White Mountains, and arrived this morning. These gentlemen are from New York ; and we were told of this festival, so as they were desirous of seeing Boston Music Hall and the school graduates, I brought them in."

"We have been repaid, for a happier set of young people is hardly ever seen," said one of the gentlemen.

They were indeed a pleasant sight to see, so bright and gay, enjoying life to the utmost. After a short time they bade good day to the young ladies, hoping to meet them again.

"What a lovely girl the one with the golden curls is!"

"Yes, and your little friend was very sensible, not at all silly like some girls."

"I guess the one with blue eyes is full of fun; she looked as if she just enjoyed a good time."

"They were all very pleasing; so natural, yet well trained, and I think Boston girls are a credit to the Hub."

"Oh, my!" said Kitty, "how nice they are! Quite put you in the shade, boys."

"Well, you just wait until we get grown up, then you will see," said Hugh.

"Never mind, we think you are our best friends, and shall claim you as our gallants for many long years," said Etta.

"Yes, indeed, an old friend is the best friend, after all," added Frances.

So they laughed and chatted until the hour came that should end this charming day.

"I don't believe we shall ever have such nice times in any other school, and I wish we could have Mr. Babcock for our teacher until we have finished our school days," said Frances, as she was telling mamma of the good success the day had been.

"He has been a good friend to 'our girls,' and you must all try to do him honor in school and in the world, as you go on in life," said papa.

"I have had such a happy life, and I think Boston is the very best city to grow up in, that I know of."

"You are a down-east girl, but still you may claim Boston as your city. The schools, churches, art-galleries, and the many advantages to be found here, are all open to those who dwell within its limits."

"Also strangers are made welcome to its many privileges," added Mr. Grey.

The girls were now able to enjoy going to lectures, concerts, and visiting the different art-museums in and about the city. They often spent many a pleasant hour in viewing the beautiful paintings in the store of Williams & Everett, which for many years has been noted for its fine collection of pictures. Thus they were gaining knowledge and a taste for the beautiful, which would add a grace to their young life. So time went on, the dark clouds which had dimmed the prosperity of the country had risen, and a new light was shining.

Ed. was now a college boy, gallant and gay. He was proud of his home, and delighted to

bring his friends for a visit in vacation. He
still liked to tease Frances, as of old, but she
had grown wiser, so did not mind it very much.
He was really very fond of his sisters, and
began to appreciate Frances, who was doing so
well in her studies, and "was quite a girl," he
said. Then Pearl was growing into girlhood,
and was dearly loved by all, and gave great
promise of talent in music.

Gilmore, the musician, joined by other prominent musical people, arranged to celebrate the
peace and prosperity of the country by a " Peace
Jubilee," to be held in Boston. It was to take
months of preparation, and all musicians were
invited to assist. A chorus of singers were
called, and the ranks of the Boston choir were
rapidly filled. The interest and enthusiasm
in this festival were wonderful to see. Every
rehearsal was fully attended, and the grand
music was soon familiar to the chorus.

The girls were calling on Frances, and talking about this Jubilee. Kitty said, "I don't
think I am a very fine singer, but I shall join
that chorus."

"Not quite equal to Parepa, who is to be one
of the soloists," said Etta.

"What a great treat it will be, to hear all the

celebrated musicians, who will be at the festival."

"The singers will have to be examined before the festival, to see if they are capable of still belonging to the chorus, after the rehearsals are over."

"It seems as if one was always being examined for something; I really get tired of it," said Frances.

"That is the way in life, we must show to the world that we can do well what we undertake, before our worth is recognized," said Mr. Grey.

"Well, I know I shall tremble when the time comes, for the music is very hard."

"I shall be so frightened that my voice will *squeak* when I attempt to sing," laughed Kitty.

"I guess we shall pass, for we can't help but know the music perfectly by that time," said Mary.

"Oh! you will be all right, for you are always perfect, but this poor child is only second best, while you are first," said Kitty.

"You flatterer, do be quiet, for you know I am no better than you are. We must try to do our best, and that is all we can do."

"A very wise conclusion, my dear Mary, and a good rule to follow," said papa.

"I think it is just glorious to sing with so many, and hear the music swell out in the chorus. I enjoy the rehearsals immensely, and Zerrahn is so full of life and spirit, one can't help but sing when he leads."

"What will it be, when all the performers are together in the Coliseum? It is to be an immense building, capable of holding thousands of people. Every one seems crazy over this Jubilee, and probably there will not be any too much space. I guess it will not seem like quiet Boston, when the musicians and visitors from all parts of the country take possession of the Hub," said mamma.

It was even so, and as the season approached the enthusiasm increased. The time for examination had come, and the girls said they must summon up their courage and go forth to battle.

Kitty said one day, "We had better try this afternoon and know our fate. I shall be terribly disappointed not to pass the examination."

So they went to Bumstead Hall, and waited until their turn came to appear before the gentleman in charge. He welcomed them so kindly that all fear fled, and they gave proof of their ability to be members of the grand chorus.

They went home with happy hearts, and a ticket in hand, which admitted them to the Peace Jubilee.

The vast extent of the Coliseum building was packed to the utmost; the large orchestra, surrounded by members of the chorus; a sea of faces beyond, waiting expectant for the leader to raise his baton. At last, the sign given, a grand anthem is taken up by the many voices. Then a single figure, that of a beautiful woman, stands up alone on a raised platform; a silence, her voice is heard, soft, yet so distinct; the sweet tones reach the farthest point of the building. Then the voice burst out in all its full power and majesty. The applause was tremendous, as Parepa, that glorious singer, bowed to the thousands that greeted her.

"I felt a queer sensation as she was singing, like chills running up and down my back," said Kitty.

"You mean that you were thrilled with the tones of her voice?" said Mary.

"Well, I suppose so, but it was a funny feeling. How quiet every thing was while she was singing; one could have heard a pin drop," said Kitty.

"It was magnificent," said Frances.

"We shall never forget this festival. I often think that we can enjoy or appreciate only a small part of the wonders we see and hear. It is enough almost to just listen to such a glorious singer," said Mrs. Grey.

"Yes, and when others are added, and all the grand instrumental music is given, it is indeed a privilege. You young people are blessed with opportunities to improve your taste for the beautiful," added Mr. Grey. They had been talking after the concert.

On Sunday evening, a sacred concert was held, and another musical treat given. Ole Bull, that wonderful violin player, delighted all with his skill.

Frances called for Etta one afternoon, but her aunt was unwilling to have her go that day. Frances used her power of coaxing, but it did no good, and she was forced to leave Etta behind. The delay caused her to miss the other girls, and she had almost decided not to go, but a feeling of impatience and annoyance urged her on, and she concluded to venture alone, although she knew that the hour was late. So she hailed a horse-car and in due time reached the Coliseum grounds. The streets were full of carriages, and the numerous entrances were crowded with people; it was a difficult thing to arrive safely where one wished to go.

Frances felt her heart beat quickly as she vainly tried to enter the building. She at last thought of the entrance where the singers had always entered, but being rather bewildered, hardly knew where to turn. After walking quite a distance the spot was reached, but to her dismay the door was shut.

What could be done? She felt completely exhausted with the heat, excitement, and the long walk. A bright thought came into her mind. A policeman stood near the entrance, and she summoned up courage to ask him if the door could be opened.

"I am late, I know, but I should like very much to be admitted," she said, rather doubtful of his willingness to help her.

"I will see what I can do," he said as he disappeared from view.

In a few moments the large door was opened, and he smilingly invited Frances to enter. A feeling of relief came over her, and she thanked her friend warmly for his kindness. Now her courage must take her to her seat, which was quite a journey from the entrance.

She went upstairs, but did not seek her place at once. The vast building was filled to its utmost capacity. The quiet was intense; a beautiful voice broke the stillness, soft and low, yet powerful, as Adelaide Phillips, that true artist, rendered the exquisite music.

The voice ceased, and such a recognition of her art as greeted the singer was seldom heard. The voice is hushed, as is that of Parepa, and the hand that drew such sweet music from the violin is now at rest. Though gone, their influence for good is felt in the world, elevating and refining the taste for the art of music.

Frances remained quiet until the notes ceased, then as the orchestra were playing a grand selection, she made her way to her seat. The girls, Mary and Kitty, were surprised to see her appear at that late hour.

"Why did n't you meet us as usual?"

"I am just as cross as I can be about it. I called for Etta, but her aunt would n't allow her to come to-day; so that made me late. I felt so annoyed that I made up my mind to come, although I was rather afraid to venture."

She told them of her experience, and of the good policeman, who so kindly assisted her. "If ever I was thankful for any thing it was to see that door open. I was in season to hear Adelaide Phillips."

Just at that moment Frances felt a touch on her arm, and looking up saw a college friend of her brother Ed. A rosy blush came over her face, for she was so surprised, and she thought this friend very nice.

"How did you find me in this crowd?" she asked.

"I noticed you as you came in, after Adelaide Phillips had sung," he replied.

"I knew that I was very prominent, but could not get to my place any other way."

"I am very glad it happened so, for I should not have seen you otherwise."

As this was recess time they talked of college news, until the sign was given for order.

At last this delightful Jubilee was over, and a great success it proved to be. Boston city was again restored to its usual quiet, and life flowed on in the same channels.

"I wonder if we shall ever do any thing in the world,—some great good?" said Frances.

"Heigho! I don't think I shall, and I am sorry we have to think seriously now, for it's a great bother. I want to have a good time first, at any rate," replied Kitty.

"Well, I can't help wishing to accomplish something in the world, when I hear such talent."

"You must all work from day to day, trying to accomplish that which you desire. Have your aim high and look forward with courage; then you will come nearer to the standard every day," said Mr. Grey.

They had been talking the events over as they made a call on Frances. Mr. Grey was as one of them, and his words of counsel sank deep into their hearts.

A great treat was in store for Frances. Brother Ed. was to graduate from college, and she was to go with Mr. Grey to the graduation. The college was in a lovely town, nestled among the New Hampshire hills. This meant a long journey, a delightful week, pretty dresses, and a coming-out, such as she had never before experienced. To a young girl nothing is so fascinating as a peep into the outside world and a share in grown-up pleasures.

Frances was now a lovely girl, with a simplicity of manner which was her great charm. She was fair indeed, but hardly realized the fact as yet. The prospect of this outing filled her with delight. The dresses were finished, and in company with other pretty dainties for the toilet, reposed in the trunk which she was to carry. The morning came to start, and in company with Mr. Grey, Brother Ed., and a young lady friend, a sister of one of the college boys, Frances was speeding on the way to the scene, which she had so often imagined.

It was just at sunset when they arrived in the college town, which had put on its gala dress for the events of the coming week.

"This is comfortable," said Frances, as they were ushered into a nice room made ready for the guests.

"Well, I am so dusty, tired, and hungry, I can hardly tell," said her friend Esther, who was with her.

It was very pleasant, and the windows looked out upon the college green, with the buildings upon it. They felt refreshed after the dust had been removed and a nice tea enjoyed. Oh! that happy week, full of enjoyment and new experiences to the young girls, or rather young ladies.

The pleasant Sunday when all went to the college church, to hear the president give his last charge to the young men who were to leave the place, where for four years they had worked together to fit themselves to go out into the world and gain an honorable position; the prize speaking excited much interest; the concert and the reception were great events, especially to the young people.

A fine programme had been arranged for the former. All was bright and gay with lights, flowers, and the sparkling faces of the audience, as they listened to the delightful music. Frances wore her pretty summer silk, with a lovely white berage cape, and very sweet she looked.

So thought her friend of the Jubilee, who was to escort her to the concert. Brother Ed. was to be Miss Esther's gallant. A very happy group, enjoying to the utmost the pleasure before them.

After the concert ended they wended their way to the president's house, where he was to receive the seniors and their friends. What a crush it was, and Frances found herself shaking hands with him, and then before she hardly knew it, was talking with some one else, who in his turn introduced her to another senior.

She was getting tired of this, when to her relief she saw her friend coming towards her, and they wended their way into the large·

grounds about the house, which were brilliantly illuminated.   It was indeed like fairy-land.

After taking a turn or two about they went into the house again.   A small room which was only lit from the hall made a nice place in which to rest.   It seemed as if it was vacant, but on entering they found others had discovered this retreat.   The occupants proved to be Brother Ed., Miss Esther, and one of the college boys with his sister.   A mutual surprise and pleasure in thus meeting.

"This room is the president's study, and we boys are politely requested to appear here, when he wishes to talk seriously to us of our numerous faults," said Ed.

"We always dread to have such an invitation," said one of the boys.

"This might be called the scolding room, then," said Esther.

"Yes, and many times the boys have gone out from it sadder yet wiser, for the little talk with the chief," said Ed.

The hour was getting late, and the company bade good night to the worthy president and his family.

"What a delightful time we have enjoyed! I shall have to pinch myself to make sure that

I am not dreaming. How much I shall have to tell the girls when I get home! I wish they were all here to have a share in this lovely week," exclaimed Frances to Esther, as they were talking over the pleasure of the evening.

Then followed Class Day, lovely walks, rides, a promenade concert in the mammoth tent which had been placed on the Common; then Commencement Day, when the graduating class received their diplomas. They would now go out into the world and make a position, using the knowledge gained, in their life work.

It was with regret that Frances found herself speeding away from this scene of pleasure. Boston was reached in due time, and she now could live it all over again in describing to the girls the delights of college life.

" I have always had so much to enjoy, but I really think this was the best of all."

"Did Ed. do well in his part at Commencement?"

"Yes, indeed! and i felt so proud to think he was my brother."

We are always glad if our friends are successful, and especially if our very own receive honors.

" Papa says that the young people of to-day have so many advantages, so different from the olden times, that they ought to accomplish a great deal."

Brother **Ed.** said to Mrs. Grey, "I tell you what, mother, Frances was one of the prettiest girls there, if she was my sister. All the fellows liked her immensely. They said she was sensible, something more than mere fuss and feathers like so many of the girls we see."

"I am very glad our girl was a credit to us. I have always known that Frances was a dear child, and would make a lovely woman," said mamma.

Although these particular girls enjoyed so many privileges and blessings, they had been taught to think of others and do their share to help those about them. Frances was with her papa a great deal and knew all of his people, who were often in need of sympathy and aid. She was a great favorite among them and received a warm welcome whenever she went to their homes. Her interest in the work of doing good was always fresh, and never abated as she grew older.

The story of living is much alike with all, but every life has its own record. If the pages can be clean and without blemish, its influence will never die.

IX.

A GLIMPSE OF THE WORLD.

THE country was now in full tide of prosperity, and America's name was respected at home and abroad. A great celebration had been planned, to take place at the close of one hundred years of American Independence. It was to be called the Centennial Exposition, and all countries were invited to send their products and manufactures, to be placed side by side with our own, thus showing how nearly equal the young republic had become to the older countries. Instantly the idea was taken up, and the people came forward to carry it out to a successful end. The city of Philadelphia was to be the centre, and vigorous preparations were made at Fairmount Park, to complete the buildings needed for this exhibition.

Frances hardly dared to hope that she might take this journey. "It will be so expensive, and I want papa and mamma to go surely," she said.

"You can keep house and take care of Pearl while they are away," replied Mary.

"Would n't it be nice if we could go together?"

"Oh! I wish we could."

"Perhaps I can go with you," said Kitty.

"That would be fine!"

"Now, mamma, I will stay at home and take good care of every thing, if you will only go."

"We will ask papa, and let him decide."

Mr. Grey's decision was that he and his wife should take the journey first, and arrange for them later, if all was well. The plan was carried out, and they came back so delighted with all they had seen, they felt as if the children *must* have the same privilege.

The day was set towards the last of September, and the girls, Mary, Kitty, and Frances, were just wild with delight. The idea of taking sole care of themselves was a novel one, which they much enjoyed. They were to go to New York by the Fall River line, and a friend was to meet them there. After spending a week in New York, they were to wend their way to Philadelphia, where a boarding-place had been engaged. The way was made plain as possible, but of course this was their first great venture alone.

They were each to take a valise, a thick shawl, and one extra dress; these, with a pretty travelling suit, made up a nice convenient outfit. Mr. Grey, Brother Ed., and Hugh went to the depot to see them off.

"Now, sis," Ed. said, "keep a level head on you, and do n't be afraid to ask questions."

"You need n't worry about that, for we can talk fast enough," laughed Kitty.

"Well, Frances is a sober young lady, so she will keep you straight," said Hugh.

"We wanted to try our fortune in the world forlorn and alone," added Mary.

"If we have good luck we may go over the seas some day," finished Frances.

The long train was packed with people, so they had plenty of company. It was about ten o'clock in the evening, when they arrived at the steamboat wharf. The cabin was now full, but they soon obtained mattresses, on which they spread their shawls, and very glad were they to rest quietly, for the boat was now rolling from side to side.

"I do feel dreadfully!" a strange voice cried out.

The girls laughed. "I guess we are not the only ones who feel queer," said Frances.

After morning lunch they were soon wrapped in their shawls and on deck. The fresh salt air blew in their faces, so refreshing after being shut up in the close cabin all night. The sun was just appearing on the horizon, lighting up the sky, which was becoming blue, with fleecy white clouds upon it; also the water, about every dancing wave reflecting back the rosy glow. A soft haze over all made the sail-boats look like tiny specks on the water.

Frances, drawing in long breaths of the delicious breeze, and feasting her eyes on the scene, said, "Can any thing be more lovely than this?"

"How beautiful, yet unreal, all this seems!" answered Mary.

"We can't enjoy these wonders half enough," sighed Frances. "Oh! I do hope our friend will be waiting for us. I have the directions to find the way, but still New York is such a world in itself that I get confused thinking of it."

As they went up New York harbor, vessels of all sizes and descriptions were seen. As the city was approached little ferry-boats darted hither and yon in all directions. At last the wharf was reached, which was also crowded with people and teams of all descriptions.

"We must look out for Mr. Lynde. I would n't miss him for any thing."

These remarks were made at intervals by the girls, as they neared their destination. Suddenly Frances cried, "There is my friend, and he sees us."

"Which one is he?"

"The gentleman waving his hat."

She waved her hand in return, and presently they were off the boat, shaking hands with him. Mr. Lynde, followed by the girls, made a dash across the platform of a horse-car and gained the other side of the street, which led into a broader avenue. Then taking a horse-car to Fulton ferry, and another one after crossing, they found themselves at last in his hospitable home, where a warm welcome was given to the strangers.

A week of sight-seeing in New York, a trip to Central and Prospect parks, a visit to the stores, a ride up famous Broadway, with its ever-changing sights, were all enjoyed by the friends.

Monday morning they found themselves in

the Jersey depot, ready to start for Philadelphia.

"I guess every one thought as we did, that Monday would be a good day to travel," said Kitty.

"We were mistaken about there not being such a crowd this morning," said Mary.

"Well, I suppose it will be just so any other day, for people are rushing now, this pleasant weather. We must keep up our courage, and I guess we shall get there safely," replied Frances.

At a given signal the doors were opened to allow the passengers to take the cars. Although the crowd was so large, they were nearly all good-natured. But as Frances was waiting to have her ticket examined a man with a valise suddenly pushed her aside, exclaiming "that he could not wait all day," and rushed by without even saying, "Excuse me." Frances hardly knew where she was for a moment, and a feeling of indignation came over her at the rudeness.

"You poor child, how awfully impolite of him!" said Mary.

"I hope we sha'n't meet many such people on the way," she answered.

Her wish was granted, as this was the only rude action they saw during the whole trip. The cars bore them rapidly onward, and in a few hours they arrived in West Philadelphia.

"I declare, girls, I hardly know what to do first, do you?" said Frances, looking about the mammoth depot, and at the crowds of people flocking into the street.

"We will ask a policeman the way to F street; that is where we are going to board," said Mary.

"We have come so far to the big time, and now we must press forward," added Kitty.

Asking one of the guardians of the city, he kindly directed them, saying it was only a square or two below here.

"That is fine! How fortunate we are to be so near, for opposite are Fairmount Park and the buildings of the Exposition."

So they started in the direction pointed out and went on, one square after another, inquiring at every corner if F street was near.

"A block or two down"; then "three or four streets," and F street was found, but the number of the house they were looking for could not be seen.

After wandering about, Frances stopped with

a sob in her voice, saying, "Well, I am tired to death; now what can we do?"

"We must stay somewhere, for we have come to see the wonders, and they must be seen before we return to Boston," said Kitty.

They walked on, but felt as if they were really lost, as they turned another street.

"This will never do, we must go back again." Just as they turned a gentleman came forward, and asked where they wished to go. On being told, he at once guided them to a house which had been passed a dozen times, and the door was opened by a pleasant-faced woman, who welcomed them kindly. Their hearts, which had been heavy, now were light, and the kind gentleman received a vote of thanks from them.

"I began to wish myself safe at home, when I thought we were lost in this big city, so far away from home and friends."

"Yes, it is not a pleasant feeling to be cast away, but one always finds kind-hearted people, who are ready to help them in any trouble," replied Mary.

"Even Robinson Crusoe, on a desert island found a man Friday," laughed Kitty.

Confidence in their ability to find the way had returned, and they gaily started out towards the park. Paying the admission fee, they were now able to view the curiosities collected from all parts of the earth. The girls were awe-struck at the task before them, to appreciate all the wonders here collected.

"Where do you suppose we ought to go first? That sign says main building, and we can investigate the sights there."

So they entered, but hardly knew which way to turn, it was so large. As they proceeded, a space devoted to Norway and Sweden was seen, and lovely furs, quaint costumes, and a Norwegian family were the attractions. A Swiss cottage with its pretty ornamental designs and curious sloping roof was next in view.

A luxurious corner the Turkish exhibit made, fitted up with soft oriental rugs and furs scattered about, with real Turks in attendance, dressed in costume, giving one an idea of the love for beautiful and gorgeous things which the Turkish people possess.

The Japanese collection was indeed a bright spot in which to rest and gaze upon the wonders from Japan. A Chinese mandarin, or merchant, had charge of the Chinese exhibit; also of the carvings in ivory of temples, pagodas, and other curious articles; fans covered with quaint figures, each representing some idea or story; rich China silks, all specimens of their wonderful skill.

Russia had sent rich furs, articles of gold and silver, tables of malachite, and models of curious carriages and sleighs, which are used in that country of ice and snow.

England had a fine assortment of her manufactures in steel, iron, and woolen goods; Queen Victoria and her daughters sending their jewels.

France was gay with rich silks, gloves, and fancy articles of every kind.

India, Prussia, South America, North America, and Europe were all represented.

The United States, although young in years, had brought forward a splendid exhibit. Each state and territory had sent manufactures of all kinds, and the natural products in minerals were wonderful.

The graceful reindeer, the polar bear, the elk, had come from the northern countries. In fact the whole building was full of curiosities from all parts of the globe.

The girls roamed about from one place to another, like butterflies, but at last they became so tired that a rest must be taken. So they sat down on one of the circular seats, and amused themselves by watching the people as they passed by.

The girls were ready to depart, having filled their minds with all they could well enjoy and remember for one day. The next morning they were up bright and early, ready for a start, and again found themselves within the charmed circle.

"Now we must choose, girls, just where we shall spend the time, so not to waste a minute," said Mary.

"I should like to see Machinery Hall," replied Frances.

"We can visit that and some of the smaller buildings to-day."

"Yes, and to-morrow take in the Art Gallery, Agricultural Hall, and perhaps others. There are so many things to see, and so many ways to go, one hardly knows what to do first."

"We must be sure to find the New England log cabin, and have some baked beans and brown bread," added Kitty.

The girls laughed at her. So talking, they wended their way to Machinery Hall. A great buzz and whirr met their ears on entering, and machinery of all kinds was in motion in every direction.

Walking to the centre of the building, they saw the great Corliss engine, which was the power that gave life to these machines. President Grant and Dom Pedro II, Emperor of Brazil, had set this engine in motion, on the opening day.

But Frances always wandered back to watch the great engine, going on and on without cessation. " It is so wonderful and seems as if it must breathe. When that stops all motion is done. Yes, like the *heart* that throbs on for years, but at last is still, and a life goes out," said Frances.

" I think you are getting serious," jested Kitty.

"Well, we are old enough now to think in earnest, and I have a curious feeling when I look at that wonderful invention. I could watch it for hours and never get tired, it is so perfect."

"Well, you can feast your eyes on *that*, but we will hunt up some dinner, and have a feast on oysters, if we can get any."

" I do feel rather oyster hungry myself," laughed Frances, "so I will go with you."

Kitty Lee was so very hungry and faint that, after being served, she seemed to forget every one else for a few moments, and was eating very fast. A young man just opposite, who had probably felt the same haste, but who had now almost finished his lunch, began to smile at her evident relish of the oyster stew. Frances and Mary noticed his amusement. After a short time Kitty looked up, and saw the funny side of the situation, and a hearty laugh was given by all.

"I never was so famished in all the days of my life," she said, "and I am going to have another stew, for it is fine! Well, I suppose I did look comical, hurrying so; it was enough to make any one laugh."

As they were dressing, the next morning, Frances remarked, "We must make good use of our time, for this is our third day, and we have only three days more in which to view the wonders of the world."

"I feel as if my head was about as full of new ideas as it could well be, but still we are here to view the scene, so we must go on gazing," added Kitty.

It was agreed that the Art Gallery or Memorial Hall should be visited that morning. This building was magnificent, being the finest on the grounds. It was built of stone, surmounted by a large statue of Columbia, and the entrance —a broad flight of stone steps—was ornamented by fine statues. This was erected by the state of Pennsylvania and the city of Philadelphia, as a permanent structure.

It contained apparently every thing rich and rare in the way of art. The collection of pictures was placed in different departments, as English, French, Italian, American, and so on. One of the most striking pictures was Rizpah, of old Bible times, watching her sons, who had been killed by a cruel king.

The girls walked about until they were utterly weary. Although resting at intervals, it was very tiresome work, and they must turn away from these fine creations for that day.

"After all that sight-seing I should enjoy some brown bread and beans," said Kitty. "Let us wend our way to the log cabin."

This was a real old-fashioned New England log cabin, and was a great attraction. As usual, a crowd was gathered there, but a table was secured, and a savory lunch was placed before them. After partaking of this, various mementos of olden times,—chairs, tables, clocks, dressers, on which bright pewter dishes were placed, also a cradle,—were to be seen, showing the way our fathers lived, when first this country was settled by them.

As they entered the main building, Kitty suddenly exclaimed, "Why! I believe that is Etta Kendall coming towards us!"

"Can it be possible?"

In a moment Etta, for it was she, rushed towards them.

"How did you happen to come?"

"When did you arrive?"

"I have been here two days, but as I did n't know your address I could n't hunt you up. I am delighted to see you, for I began to think you must have departed. I am with some friends of aunt's—a lady and gentleman—who were stopping with us. Aunt said that I had been so faithful this summer in helping her, I deserved a vacation. So here I am, and how splendid it is we can be together once more!"

"Have you seen the handsomest man in the exhibition?" said Kitty Lee.

"Pray, who is he, and where can he be seen?" replied Etta.

"In the Chinese corner; he is a Chinese mandarin and is just gorgeous!"

So thither they went, and all agreed with Kitty, for this merchant dressed in his robes was a very fine-looking Chinaman.

"I come here every day to have a look at him, and I guess all the ladies admire him, for there is always a crowd around," said Kitty.

"Oh! you are very gushing, Kitty, but he is handsome, that can't be denied," laughed Mary. "I propose we visit Horticultural building this afternoon, for it is not so tiresome looking at flowers and fruits."

"What a fairy-land this is! Can one even imagine the lovely and endless variety of shrubs and blossoms?" Frances said. "I am going to sit by this fountain and just gaze, for I am too tired to walk about."

Mary kept her company, and they rested on a seat, which was surrounded by tropical plants of immense size, and other specimens whose blossoms threw out delightful perfume.

"We can hear the organ concert in the main building before we go away," said Frances.

So all the party returned to that place, and listened to a very fine programme.

"Come and take tea with us, and we can arrange for to-morrow," said Mary.

So their friends went with them, and a pleasant evening was spent.

"We can meet at the grand stand in the morning, visit as many points of interest as possible, then I will engage a carriage for the afternoon, and change the scene by driving around the city," said the gentleman friend.

"That will be splendid! Let us hunt up Independence Hall, where the Declaration was signed. We have seen the original document, which is on exhibition. It is yellow with age, but is carefully guarded from all harm."

At an early hour, good-night was said, and they retired. The promise was kept, and they all arrived at the grand stand, about the same time.

Entering at once the Woman's Pavilion, they were soon absorbed in this exhibit of the industry of women.

Etta said, "I am really discouraged, when I look at all these beautiful things, to think how little I can do."

"I do n't think you need to feel so, for you are capable about every thing. I wish I could do half as much as you can," answered Mary.

"There are not many girls like Etta, but we

must try to fit ourselves to be of some use in our little world," replied Frances.

"Oh! girls, you are always longing to do so much. I am just now ready to leave all these wonders and hunt up a lunch room," jested Kitty. "We might see how the French live to-day."

They were all willing, so went to the French restaurant. It was a costly plan, and they voted that once was enough.

"Give me old-fashioned brown bread and beans, for I do n't feel as if I had eaten half enough, but my allowance in that line is spent to-day," exclaimed Kitty.

"Very nice style, but not quite enough to eat. We have a hearty supper in prospect," said Frances.

Mr. R—— now was waiting for them, just outside the gates, and they were soon driving along the banks of the Schuylkill river. Then Girard College was visited, and the view from this point, as the city, Fairmount Park, and surrounding country could be seen, was magnificent.

Coming to the city itself, the houses looked rather odd, with their white blinds and high stone steps. They visited a number of public buildings, and saw the old hall in which the "Fathers" met to sign the freedom of the United States. The afternoon had gone speedily away, and they all were sorry when darkness overtook them. This trip had been one of the delights, for they had enjoyed so much, but did not become weary.

Mary said, "Philadelphia is a fine place, but my heart turns to Boston."

"Yes, there is no place like home. I don't think if one roamed the world over any city could be found that was quite so nice as Boston,—so comfortable-like," added Frances.

"We all agree in that, and shall always shout for the 'Hub,'" cried Kitty.

Etta was to stay with the girls that night, and the next day, which was the last, must be well employed in trying to see all they had passed by. Agricultural Building was visited at once, and the girls began to realize the importance of farming and producing food for the millions, who were waiting for the products. The western states had sent a noble offering of grain, which was arranged in various shapes. Gold quartz from California.

"Girls, here is the naval exhibit of guns and every thing used in war, and models of ships.

We must tell the boys, for they would like to see this collection."

"I shall never forget this trip as long as I live, and I feel so glad that I could come and enjoy it all," said Frances.

"It is almost too good to be true," said Etta.

"I feel just like giving three cheers for the Centennial, but I am afraid it might make a commotion," said Kitty.

As they were very weary, a rest was needed before taking the journey home. Mary, Kitty, and Frances were to go directly to Boston, and Etta was to stop with her friends in New York. The next morning, as the cars steamed out of the depot, a group of girls with smiling faces stood on the platform of one, taking a last look at the Centennial city, where so many happy hours had been spent in storing their minds with a knowledge of the world.

After this trip the girls settled down again to daily work at home and in school. As time went on they continued to advance higher, and the way opened to new fields of work, and life lay before them in all its brightness. They had been guided and taken care of by kind friends, while so many about them had been left to find the rough side of life with all its hardships.

Frances said to her papa, as she entered the library one evening after studying the next day's lessons, "I have been thinking that it was time for me to decide just what I can do, after my school days are over."

"Well, my dear, circumstances will probably decide that question, but I think you have a talent for writing, which will become stronger the more you use it."

"I think girls should fit themselves for some practical work."

"Yes, and study to improve any talents given them," said papa. "Now Pearl is musical, and she can cultivate that line, for music is always in demand."

"I know I can be a musician if I try, and a good one, I hope," chimed in Pearl.

"But I think I shall be a journalist and write for the newspapers," said Frances.

"Foreign correspondent?" laughed Ed.

"You needn't laugh, for I may be one some day, nobody knows."

"I hope my children will all strive to do their very best in the world," said mamma.

"Improve the shining hours as they go, and you will have your reward," said Mr. Grey.

X.

THE OTHER SIDE.

WONDERS never cease. So thought two young girls—one somewhat older than the other—as they stood on the deck of a large steamer which was to cross the Atlantic ocean. It was a "misty, moisty" morning, and as these sisters—for they were such— saw their native shores recede from view, the watching friends fade from sight, the mist seemed to gather in their eyes, and they turned away to the friends who were to be companions for the voyage. Still it was a very delightful plan which was to be carried out, even if a feeling of sadness came over them at this time.

It had just happened—this joy—and they hardly realized yet the journey before them, but knew that this trip was to be one of profit as well as pleasure. It seemed hardly possible that they were the same girls, who a few years before had talked over plans for the future, in that pleasant library with the dear papa, who gave them such good advice.

"You will be led, my children, in the right way," he said.   Yes, the dream had come true, and Frances Grey and her sister Pearl were now passengers on the good ship, which was rapidly carrying them to the other side.   "Dear old home, we must keep up its honor, when we reach a foreign shore."

They were indeed two fine-looking girls, intelligence beaming in their faces; bright yet modest ways, which always gain respect; they would be favorites anywhere.   Frances had studied faithfully, and earned the position she desired, and was now to add knowledge of other countries, that her pen might fashion words into interesting form.

Pearl was to have the advantage of instruction from the best musicians abroad.   She was to keep a journal of the voyage, and in due time, a letter was going back over the water, while each day was taking them on to the shores of "Merrie England."

Thursday, 7 P.M.

IN THE MUSIC-ROOM OF THE GOOD SHIP.

My Blessed Mother and All my Friends :

I have just succeeded in eating a hearty dinner, and am feeling splendidly: have not been a bit sick. It is gay fun so far.

Friday.—Well, another day has gone. It has been clear and smooth. This morning I was a bit seasick, but I dressed in a hurry and made for the deck, leaving poor Frances to the care of the good stewardess, who had insisted on my taking some tea and toast. I felt decidedly the worse for wear until 11 A. M.; then I had a cup of beef tea and two crackers, then a lunch and a hearty dinner. The sunset to-night was magnificent. There are some lovely people on board, and we have great fun. A *real lord*, who lives in London, a perfect Englishman, very polished in his manners. I am at the table with the captain and the purser. The purser is "awfully swell,"—English. We have animated talks at dinner between Lord S—— and the purser, who always disagree, on principle. The missionaries are finely educated people, who are giving their lives to teach the heathen in the interior of Turkey. Oh, dear! I am afraid I could n't do it. Frances has disappeared from public view. I feel so sorry for her, but hope she will improve.

Saturday.—Another beautiful day, it has been simply perfect, and I have not felt a qualm. Have eaten like a pig and sleep like one at night. Frances says in a faint voice, "Give the folks my love," and then sinks back to misery.

Sunday.—To-day, at 10 : 30 A. M., we held a service in the saloon. The purser read the Episcopal service, and all the sailors came in. I led the singing and played the piano. As we sang the old familiar hymns, "Jesus, Lover of my Soul," and "Nearer, my God, to Thee," I could not help thinking, that although one might go away into foreign countries, still the same loving care is present, and one finds the same faith everywhere.

Thursday.—A week to-day on shipboard; it seems a

year. You see, there is not very much variety, and we have been hunting after some new amusement. We are only five hundred miles from Queenstown. I dread the custom-house officers, but I shall put on my sweetest smile. Frances went up on deck to-day and wishes the voyage could last a week longer, she feels so fine.

The lovely shores of Ireland were covered with fog when they reached Queenstown. Liverpool, that long-looked-for city, was reached early in the morning, and they went with their friends at once to the custom house. A kindly young man looked over their trunks, but as Pearl had said "she should put on her sweetest smile, and help him to examine them," he was very good, although he looked rather suspiciously at a tin box of Kennedy's ginger snaps. Pearl opened it and gave him one; he laughed and closed the trunk satisfied.

"Well, Pearl, that was nicely done; I hope we shall meet with so much politeness everywhere," said Frances.

After lunch they took the train to London. The girls were perfectly delighted with the scenery; such green meadows and hills; small cottages with thatched roofs; here and there a castle of gray stone, with a tower. Every inch of ground seemed well cultivated. London was reached in the afternoon, and they went at once to the boarding-place which had been engaged. The lady of the house warmly welcomed them, showing them to a pleasant room, which looked out upon a lovely square.

"I tell you, Pearl, the sight of that good New England face,—for you know, this lady is from Boston,—has almost cured this homesick feeling which has been tugging away at my heart-strings ever since we left our friends," said Frances. She had been looking a bit serious.

"Oh! we must n't be homesick," said Pearl bravely. "We shall be all right to-morrow, I guess. Of course we shall, and I think this will be a lovely home," said Pearl.

"What a vast place London is! I do n't believe we shall ever learn our way about," said Frances.

"Well, here we are, with a winter before us, in which to discover *all* that is interesting," answered Pearl.

A nice home indeed they had found; the house was opposite a pretty green park, with seats and fountains, green trees and flowers. This residence was of gray stone, six stories high, with a big front door having a knocker on it. Every morning, a street band played for an hour under their windows, much to the delight of Pearl, who could never practise until they were done, "for music hath charms to soothe the savage breast," she said. Although so many miles from their own country, it seemed like home, as the family were mostly Americans who had also found this fine stopping-place. Coming from different parts of America, still their interests were the same, and the enthusiasm for the "Land of the Free" never failed. London was indeed a vast place; one might live there for months and not see half of the sights of this immense city. But these girls were of an inquiring mind and meant to see all they possibly could.

"I am sure, I didn't come across that big ocean just for the journey. I mean to learn all I can of the world," said Frances.

In this Pearl heartily agreed, and in a few weeks was earnestly engaged in her musical studies. Frances devoted her time to study suited to her work, and daily visited some new portion of London, gathering up ideas of the way people lived and of famous places, which can hardly be counted on this little isle. The October weather was lovely, but they were told

THE TOWER OF LONDON.

that London would soon be given up to fog and rain, so they must now go about while it was fine.

One day, very much to their delight, a party of friends, who had been on ship-board, came to see them. At once plans were made for sight-seeing, and this was the result: A friend had obtained passes from the governor of the Tower, and they were admitted to places where the general public never go. Going up the river Thames in a boat, a fine view of all the wharves of London, Billingsgate Market, and Blackfriars Bridge was obtained. The Tower of London is a marvellous place. They saw the magnificent crown jewels; the scaffold; St. Peter's chapel, where all the victims were buried; the room where the young princes were smothered; all the armor; the rack; thumb-screw; block, axe, and mask of headsman; the dark, gloomy dungeons underneath the Tower; a cell, called "Little Ease," just large enough for a man to stand or sit, but not to lie down, — Guy Fawkes was kept there six weeks, — The Traitor's Gate, a noted place; in one room inscriptions on the walls, where the prisoners carved their names.

As Pearl said, "My blood fairly ran cold when

I heard who had been imprisoned in those horrible places."

The next day, to do away with the gloomy impression made by the visit to the Tower, they went to see Madame Tussaud's waxworks. It was well worth a 6*d.* to see them. They are life-size figures, arrayed in elegant dresses, and arranged in groups. Among them were Irving, Ellen Terry, all the kings and queens, the entire royal family, Lincoln, Grant, Garfield, statesmen, and the beautiful queen regent and infant king of Spain. The girls could hardly believe that they were of wax, they looked so life-like.

"Why, these people are in full dress! Look at that old man, turning his head around, viewing the scene," they said, and were astonished at the deception.

After this trip these friends flitted away to warmer climes, for the winter.

Pearl said, "I begin to like London, even if it is dingy and smoky."

"How nice it is that we find the English people so friendly! I think they are very cordial," replied Frances.

"I know we shall have a splendid time at this party we have been invited to attend. Out at the famous Hampstead Heath, we can see what English hospitality—that is a long word—is, and I have always been eager to be right in it," said Pearl.

"I have always liked so much to read books

READY FOR SIGHT-SEEING.

describing this life, and now can see for myself," answered Frances.

So, at the appointed time, they arrived at Hampstead, one of the prettiest suburbs of London. Pearl had said,— "Now we must dress our very finest; I shall wear my black silk skirt and pink satin waist, and I think that will do"; but the girls found that they were the plainest dressed of any at the party.

Pearl wrote home, "The family where we visited live in splendor! Oh! how the English girls do dress! But they are very quiet, not at all talkative, very different from American girls.

"We enjoyed a delightful evening, such as an English host knows how to provide. The next morning we went for a fine walk, up to the famous ''Amstead 'eath, where 'Arry and 'Arriot go on a bank holiday,' ready for sight-seeing, and it was a very interesting and instructive walk to us.

"This heath is a vast valley, covered with prickly gorse, and is the road from Highgate to London. In olden times no one dared cross Hampstead Heath after sundown, for it was full of highwaymen. So travelers would put up at the Spaniards' Inn, just on the borders of the heath. It is a funny place and looks as if it was very ancient.

"We saw the woods where Guy Fawkes was discovered in hiding, at the time of the Gunpowder Plot; we saw the homes of John Keats, William Pitt, Hannah More, and Thomas Hood. In fact, Hampstead Heath is a charming place, well worth seeing.

"We received a great deal of kindness, being invited to visit this family whenever we wished. Now don't think we are neglecting our studies with all this pleasure. We study first and then have a good time."

One day Pearl burst into the room where Frances was quietly writing, exclaiming, "Oh! Oh! Oh!"

"Why, what is the matter!" said Frances, alarmed.

"Only think, my dear master has given me two tickets to hear Patti sing! Now you can go, and that will be fine!"

So the news was told, and a party from the house arranged to go with them. They took a carriage, which cost them three shillings apiece, and their seats were in a stall or box. The concert was in Albert Hall, which is like a vast amphitheatre.

As Frances said, "dear old Music Hall was only a little room in comparison; but give me that home-like place for real enjoyment." This Albert Hall was filled to overflowing, and all the people in full evening dress. Royalty abounded, and it was a magnificent occasion. Patti sang three times, being called back each time. She gave three opera airs, "Last Rose of Summer," "Within a Mile of Edinboro' Town," "Comin' thro' the Rye," "Home, Sweet Home," and a duet with Nicolini. At her last appearance that evening, the people rose and cried, " Bravo! '"

The girls were wild over Patti. As Frances said, " she just opens her mouth and sings like a bird ; her execution is wonderful!" Her dress of pink silk and the jewels she wore were elegant.

It was difficult to find their carriage, but they arrived home at twelve o'clock, highly delighted with the treat.

They were invited to join a party to visit Hampton Court. It was a bright clear day, and they took the underground railroad to Portland Road, then a "bus" to Waterloo Station, and a train to Teddington, and entered Bushby Park, which was enchanting, walking a mile through long avenues of oak trees, with deer running about under the trees; going around a lake with swans on the water, they passed through a large gate and found themselves at Hampton Court.

They went to the " King's Arms " to lunch, a typical English inn, built of stone, with a pretty bar-maid and a very obsequious waiter; it was purely English. As they were eating a lunch of tea, bread, butter, and marmalade, the coach drove up, fresh horses were put in, and away it went, with blowing of horns and a great fuss about nothing.

After this they at once entered the gate of Hampton Court. This palace was built by Cardinal Wolsey, and presented by him to King Henry VIII. It is an enormous building built of red brick, with battlemented walls. There are three courts: the entrance court, the clock court, and the fountains court. These courts are within each other, each gate guarded by armed soldiers. The King's Grand Stairway is adorned with pictures by Verrio. The king's apartments are the premier and audience chambers, the drawing-room, the bed-room of King William III, in which is a clock which only needs winding up once a year. The walls of the whole suite of rooms are covered by paintings, done by Titian, Rubens, Guido, and Correggio, also the Court Beauties and all sorts of curiosities. Outside are the most magnificent gardens; a grape-vine one hundred and eighty years old, which bears twenty-five hundred bunches of grapes every year, also an avenue of one hundred trees, called Queen Anne's Walk, are some of the attractions.

So the lovely day passed in visiting these

spots, and they arrived at home at half-past six, having made a whole day of it.

The weather now had become rainy, and the strangers found that waterproofs and umbrellas were needed on every occasion. However, they were not to be kept from going to points of interest. At one time they visited Westminster Abbey. The grandeur of this church, the beautiful music, and the stillness of the old abbey quite awed them. Frances said, "I fancied I was away back a hundred years or more, the whole place was so ancient."

After the service the party went to the tombs, where the kings and queens are buried, among them Mary and Elizabeth, and all the prominent men of the kingdom. Also saw the chair which is used when the kings and queens are crowned.

At another time they attended service at St. Margaret's church. This is one of London's finest churches. The Prince of Wales and his family attend here. The church is magnificent, with stained-glass windows and a superb altar. Candles were burning, a choir of sixty boys sang divinely, and the service was very inspiring.

The Zoological Gardens were very interesting. The grounds are beautifully laid out, and animals of all sorts and kinds, — bears, kangaroos, and serpents, — are to be seen. " Jumbo," so well known to Americans through the energy of Barnum, was kept here many years.

In their daily walks curious sights were seen. A rich lady leading a poodle dog by a gold chain; then a poor, ragged beggar woman, with a baby in her arms, two or three little children hanging to her skirts, she singing some doleful melody about "being homeless," asking for a penny; next a man painting pictures on the paving-stones in the street, people going by throwing him a penny; then a stout peasant woman with a yoke on her shoulders, and suspended from that two enormous cans of milk; she would be dressed in a short, red and blue gown, with a cap on her head; then a poor idiot sitting on the street-corner, an object of pity. It was really heart-rending, and the girls could never become used to these pitiful sights.

In a letter home Frances said, " A few mornings ago we commenced to hear sung in the street, 'I remember, I remember, the fifth of November,' by many groups of men and boys. It was Guy Fawkes' day, and the anniversary of the famous Gun-powder Plot. Before the day was over, we wished Guy Fawkes had never been born. I was writing in the drawing-room, when I heard a loud noise in the street. A crowd of ragamuffins were dragging a cart, in which was placed an effigy of Guy Fawkes, life size, dressed in royal splendor, wearing a light wig and peaked hat, with a mask for a face· The men were howling out this pathetic ditty: 'Guy Fawkes! Guy! Hang him to a lamp-post, and there let him die!' Then they expected you to open the window and give them a penny. This was kept up at intervals during the day, and in the evening all the Guys were burned in a field.

"Yesterday was Lord Mayor's Day, which is the great show for the year in London. It is when the new lord mayor comes into office, and an enormous procession of all the trades and the state carriages parade the streets. We did not see it, as the socialists threatened a riot, so it was thought better not to venture out. A slight affray took place in Trafalgar Square, but was quelled."

Their London home was very pleasant, and the long evenings were enlivened by music and games, candy pulls, and all sorts of frolics.

One of the gentlemen made much fun for them; "the bonny Englishman," as Pearl called him.

This gentleman was in the mining business, owning mines in Wigan. After one of his journeys to that locality, he brought Pearl some photographs of the women who work in these mines, side by side with the men.

"Poor creatures, how dreadful!" said Pearl.

"They do not look unhappy, and how strong they must be!" said Frances.

"They take their life as a matter of course, as they are brought up so from their youth," he replied.

"How true the saying is, 'that one-half of the world does not know how the other half live!'" said Frances.

Pearl gave an account of a dinner party they attended. "We supposed it was to be a small affair, so wore our woolen dresses, but found that silks and satins were the order of the day. We knew we looked well, so kept up the honor of America.

"The house was perfectly elegant,—very English—and the dinner fine. The guests were English, American, French, a lady from Belfast, Ireland, a Polish lady, who is maid of honor to Queen Charlotte, of the house of

Louis Philippe, the only surviving remnant of royalty in France. She was a perfect beauty and looked like a Spanish princess.

"An English society fop, with a dress suit, and an eye-glass in his left eye, quite amused me. He said, 'Weally, I thought Americans were quite saw-vage, don't you know.' I coolly informed him that we did n't go around with tomahawks in our hands or scalps at our belts, at which he looked blank. A prolonged stare of the eye-glass, and 'Oh!' was all he could say. It was really a laughable experience.

"A military man, Captain S——, said to me, after I had been singing, 'You must go in for singing and that sort of a thing, for you sing awfully well, you know.' He also remarked to a friend, 'that Miss Grey was really quite clever.' I was much amused by this compliment.

"We enjoyed a great treat in Lady Folkestone's concert. We had with us a Mrs. H——, who was a lovely companion. Our seats were the finest in the hall,—for my master had given them to us,—among the royalty; just think of it! I presume people thought she was Lady —— and her daughters.

" The best thing in the concert was a ladies'

string band, composed of fifty girls, taken from the nobility, and conducted by Viscountess Folkestone herself. They were all dressed in white, and the way the violins,—first, second, third,—were designated from the 'cellos, was by different-colored ribbon bows on their shoulders. The bows, red, pink, blue, and yellow, looked very pretty. The playing—well, it was grand! Lady Folkestone was dressed in mauve velvet and diamonds. She came out, baton in hand, and led those girls through several very difficult selections, with the utmost ease and composure. They were so perfectly trained that it seemed almost like one instrument.

" The vocalists were all good, and a violinist, a young Frenchman, M. Louis D'Egville, played wonderfully. He astonished the audience by playing a duet on the piano and violin at the same time; he held his violin in position with his teeth, playing it with one hand and using the other to play the piano.

"This last week we have had dreadful fogs, and are quite disgusted with November in London. Wherever you go every one is coughing and sneezing. You people at home have no idea of a London fog. All your most dreadful conceptions of it would fall short of the mark, and no pen can do it justice. It is now one o'clock, and I can hardly see to write. I look out of the window, and what do I see?—a blank wall of fog, so black that the lights in the street are not discernible. The park is hid, and I should never know there were houses on the other side of the square. I hear a team in the street, but can not tell whether it is a hackney-cab or a green-grocer's cart. The room is full of smoke or fog, rolling about. I have two burners lighted, and can see my paper a little better. It is a *black* fog to-day, which makes your eyes smart, and you feel as if you could not get your breath.

"Frances and I went out for a little while this morning. When we started it was a clear day, the sun was shining, although the air was chilly. As we reached Regent street the fog was so bad that we could n't see our hands before us. After much trouble we succeeded in getting a bus and arrived home safely. If you imagine a dozen houses on fire and yourself in the midst of the smoke, you may have a *slight* idea of what we are going through.

"One evening all the young people went to the circus. We took a four-wheeler or bathing-machine, as it is called, and rode to the building where the show is given. It is almost like a theatre, and a vast improvement upon a tent, with the rain dripping down upon you. The trained horses were beautiful, and a trained donkey that would not go out of a walk was very funny. One of the men kept trying to make him go and called him his fast trotter. One of the attendants asked him where he obtained that *noble* animal; he said, 'In America!' We had a great laugh and a fine time.

"We have visited the British Museum. To describe the wonderful antiquities, from all parts of the globe, would be impossible. Among them were the famous Elgin marbles, taken from the Parthenon at Athens; also the Rosetta Stone, which was the key to several languages; also some wonderful manuscripts.

"We are very busy with our studies, and have taken up German, with a fine teacher, as we are looking forward to our trip to Germany in the spring."

Thanksgiving Day came, and was celebrated by the family in the New England style, with turkey, chickens, plum pudding, and mince pie for dinner. In the evening they sang college songs, played games, and acted charades.

After tea and coffee had been passed round, Pearl played the "Black Art." No one could guess the secret in it, so she had to explain the plan of the game. Then as the hour grew late, they all sang "America" with a right good will.

Frances in writing home said, "One Sunday afternoon we went to St. Paul's cathedral, to hear the resident preacher, Canon Liddon. Although an hour in advance of the time for service, we had great trouble in obtaining seats, but were well repaid for our long waiting. There were nearly three thousand people in the congregation, among them many Americans.

"Cannon Liddon is a very old man, but a powerful preacher. The singing was the finest we have heard in London. They have two large organs, and a choir of boys, and when they sing a grand old anthem, it is powerful. One part of the service was sung outside, by the boys alone, and it seemed like the voices of angels, it was so sweet. St. Paul's is a vast place and, like Westminster, was very awe-inspiring to me.

"Coming home we passed Snow Hill, spoken of by Dickens, in 'Nicholas Nickleby,' as the place where Squeers used to start from to go to Dotheboy's Hall; also Newgate prison and the Old Bailey. I am glad that I am familiar with Dickens, for so many of the scenes in his books were laid in London. Some day we are to visit Dickens' haunts, places from which the different scenes in his books were taken.

"It is nearing Christmas, and we are looking forward to a *real* English Christmas. The weather is very cold, but we care little for that if the fogs do n't appear. The misery and suffering during this cold weather are terrible. So many people come under the windows and sing, ' We are starving, for we have no work to do.' Men, women, and children stand about the streets, looking half-frozen, and beg, beg, all day. It makes me sad to think I can not help the multitude, who are thus forced to ask charity. I often think of the poorer classes in Boston, and of the never-failing benevolence shown towards them.

"The Christmas Waits were singing carols last night, and all the shops are decked out in gala-dress. Our good hostess gives Christmas boxes to her tradesmen, servants, dust-man, chimney-sweep, post-man, policeman, parcel-boy, and many others.

"We have not decided where we shall spend our Christmas holidays. We have a vacation of two weeks, and feel as if a change would benefit us. But we wish you all a Merry Christmas."

The next letter which the home people received was dated, "Ventnor, Isle of Wight, Dec. 24th."

"You will doubtless be astonished when you receive this letter from Ventnor, and wonder why we came here. Well, our dear friends, Mr. and Mrs. H——, sent us an invitation to join them in Ventnor, and spend our two weeks' vacation in this lovely spot. Ventnor is one of the principal towns in the famous Isle of Wight. It is away out at sea, sheltered from the cold winds, and the air is clear and bracing. It is a noted place for invalids, and people afflicted with throat and lung troubles are always sent to Ventnor. We are to take an entire rest, and you can't imagine what a relief it is to breathe the pure sea air and not the dreadful fog.

"We started at 10:30 A. M. from London, and reached Portsmouth harbor at 1:10 P. M. We travelled third class and were very comfortable; for by giving the guard the mighty shilling, he was very attentive, and kept *guard* over us all the way. The scenery between London and Portsmouth was lovely, and after we left London the sun came out so bright. We had hardly seen its rays for weeks. We passed through the Hampshire country, with its lovely parks and old country mansions, so homelike and picturesque.

"After reaching Portsmouth harbor we took the boat to Ryde. It was a nice little trip across the Channel, of an hour and a half, past the forts and war-ships which guard the approach to England. We stayed on deck all the time, for the sea air was so invigorating. Reached Ryde, in the Isle of Wight, at 3:45 P. M., and took a train to Ventnor, arriving at 4:30 P. M.

"Mr. H—— was at the station to meet us, and a most cordial welcome we received. The house where we are staying is called St. Boniface Boarding-house. It is built of gray stone, and every thing is pure English; we have four meals a day and could eat six, only think of that! We are hungry all the time.

"Ventnor is built on terraces, and completely sheltered from the north winds by the downs, which are seven hundred and eighty feet above

the level of the sea.   These downs are perfectly green.   We went for a walk about the town
and down to the wonderful ocean.

"The town is a queer little place, with narrow, crooked streets; the houses all of stone,
covered with ivy.   The shops trimmed with
boughs of holly and mistletoe. Can you imagine
the flowers in bloom, the air mild and balmy, the
day before Christmas?   We walked down, and
down, and down, to the Esplanade, which is
the fashionable walk of the town.   It is close
by the sea, and one can walk for over a mile on
the dry pavement.   To look over the sea, at
the gorgeous sunset, then look up at the lovely
green downs, with the funny little town, its
houses built on the sides of the hills, and the
sun shining over all, was indeed glorious!

"This Christmas will be a very unique one
for us.   We often say to each other, can we be
the same girls who have lived all our lives in
the quiet New England city of Boston?   We
can hardly realize this great privilege we are
having, in seeing all these lovely spots across
the ocean.   But however beautiful, we are very
proud of our home and always say we are
American girls, with great emphasis.

"We are going to visit all points of interest

ESPLANADA, LOWESTAFF, ENGLAND.

in the island.   Queen Victoria has a winter residence here, called Osborne, and is coming
down shortly.   *We* shall receive her, of course,
and say we are very glad to see her.   No doubt
she will feel highly complimented."

'*Christmas night*, 9:15 *P. M.*—I will now
continue my letter, and tell you how we spent
Christmas Day.   Went to church in the morning.   It was beautifully trimmed with holly,
and ivy, and flowers in profusion.

"It has been a charming day, clear and bright.
The downs look so green and inviting that it re-
minded me of the old song, 'Oh! who would o'er
the downs so free,' and made me wish I was up
at the top of them.   After service we walked on
the Esplanade, which was crowded with people.
It is sad to see so many invalids, cripples, and
consumptives.   The air is invigorating, and the
warm pure wind from the sea causes one to feel
so fresh and gay.   Then we were ready to eat
the English Christmas dinner, of turkey and
plum pudding, which was just delicious.   In
the afternoon I read and covertly gazed over
my book at a pair of lovers.   She is in con-
sumption, and he came to visit her this Christmas time.   It is sad to see one so young and
beautiful fading away.   Ah! another year she

may be in her heavenly home! At five o'clock we were served with tea, bread, and butter, and at eight o'clock we had supper: cold meats, bread, cake, fruit, and wine, and bonbons with fancy caps in them. We have passed an exceedingly pleasant day, but our thoughts have often gone back to our dear home, with the hope that all was well.

" I think if Frances could have the home people and all her girls with her, she would be content to linger here forever. Well, it is the loveliest spot on earth, and I wish it could be transported, climate and all, to Boston harbor, and we could have a home within its borders; it would be enchanting. That is a very moderate wish; do n't you think so? We have both received many gifts from our friends, which is very gratifying."

" *Jan. 2d. Ventnor.*—Pearl said last night that it was my turn to write, and that I must begin the New Year by doing so. I have to prepare so much to send over the seas that I do neglect my home letters. We are still at beautiful Ventnor. I am more charmed with its loveliness every day I stay, and I dread to leave it and go back to London fog, soot, and rain. We hear that the fogs have been frightful, and there has been a snow-storm since we left, but we have not seen any snow yet. The weather here for the past week has been bright and clear. I have fairly reveled in sun, fresh air, and charming scenery.

"We have spent most of the time out of doors and walked every day to some new point of interest. One can walk many miles, the atmosphere is so bracing. The most beautiful thing about Ventnor is the vegetation. English ivy abounds, and the trunks of trees and great rocks are completely covered with it.

"We walked to Bonchurch, to see the new church just built there. It is of gray stone, and is situated in a dell, surrounded by high cliffs; these rocks are covered with ivy and noble trees, as green as in the summer. In every direction you are completely fascinated by tempting little paths, luring you on and on by their witching beauty. I plucked a dandelion in full bloom. Just fancy! English, you know.

"We went home by Bonchurch Cliff, which is far above the sea; the ocean view from that point is grand. We saw a large steamer just off the shore, and asked a sailor, who was making observations through a telescope, what she was and where bound. He said she was a

Pacific and Oriental, just starting for India. He let us look through his glass, and we could see the people on board of her.

"As Pearl has written, we walk on the Esplanade every day at least an hour. There are rather too many invalids to make it an unalloyed pleasure, for one is constantly seeing some new deformity, or the sad, pale face of some sufferer. But that is the dark side of the picture, for all the people who walk there do not come under the head of invalidism.

"We amuse ourselves by conjuring up histories of the people we meet each day. Miss W. is partly Irish, and has a great deal of fun in her merry blue eye, and we find her very amusing, saying funny things. There are two young men who haunt the Esplanade, who are very romantic-looking. Pearl says they are Spaniards, but Miss W. says they are Negroes. I heard them talking some strange language, but we are in doubt.

"I stand on the beach and look off in the direction of America, trying to fancy I can see it, but in vain. The waves come in most furiously here and dash up enraged against the enormous cliffs. I never saw such rocks in my life; they are of a pinkish color, and the reflection makes the waves a bright pink. Can you imagine first a pink, then a light blue, and away off in the distance a dark blue? I could watch this scene for hours, and never grow weary. How I wish Mary with her artistic eye could see all this loveliness! Perhaps she could catch some of the beauty on canvas, and keep it always. I can only search for *words* to describe these wonders, and fail to find them.

"Last week a fine large steamer from New Orleans, bound for Antwerp, went on the rocks at Blackgang, which is twenty miles from Ventnor. She was loaded with cotton. The sea was calm, but there was a thick fog which caused the accident. A young Englishman boarding here, much to our surprise and delight, hired a trap and invited six of us to drive to Blackgang and see the wreck. We went in fine style, with a pair of horses; we drove through woods and over the most beautiful road; on each side, lovely flowers and thick ivy running to the top of great trees. I think Dickens must have been to this isle when he wrote the 'Ivy Green.' We occasionally had glimpses of the sea, and now and then passed fine old residences. Steep Hill Castle was one of the most interesting. We stopped at a toll-gate and paid sixpence, and then went up and down hill, until we came to Blackgang, named for a gang of smugglers once quartered there. Here we saw St. Catherine's Point, with its coast-guard station and light-house, out on a rock in the sea.

"Two miles beyond, we stopped at a stile, then went over a field, jumped a ditch, and came to a cliff, where the *Cormorant* went ashore. There she was on the rocks so helpless, with the waves dashing furiously over her. We could not get near, so stood on the cliff above, and watched the sailors pull up the bales of cotton by ropes, and although one thousand bales had been taken out, they had still six thousand to bring up. Pearl made friends with one of the sailors, and he gave her a piece of the white cotton.

"From that point, we saw the 'Needles,' which are three rocks standing off the coast. They are snow-white and gleam most splendidly in the sun, and they are the first point of land seen by the North German Lloyd steamers, coming from America. A signal station is on the one nearest the land.

"After viewing the wreck, we drove to Blackgang Chine. A chine is a dell or cleft, between two rocks. Blackgang Chine is a famous one. Standing on a raised platform, we gazed down into the deep, dark ravine. We did not descend, as many people do; it seemed appalling, and we were glad to remain on the platform.

"We then drove to Ventnor and so ended our expedition to the wreck of the *Cormorant.* Pearl sang that evening, 'The Wreck of the Hesperus,' with thrilling effect.

"Every day I learn something new, and I am greedily storing away bits of knowledge for future use. I don't think Pearl mentioned the churchyard at Bonchurch, where William Adams, the author of 'The Shadow of the Cross,' is buried. Upon his grave is placed a huge iron cross, and when the sun shines upon it the shadow of this cross is seen upon the grave. This is emblematic of the book. John Sterling, mentioned so often by Carlyle, in his letters to Emerson, is also buried here. I plucked a daisy, and also a little white flower, called the Christmas rose, from his grave.

"We visited the Royal National Hospital. Instead of being one large building, it is seven or eight stone cottages, built on a high cliff, facing the sea. These cottages have been built by wealthy people from London. It is under the patronage of Her Majesty, and the work is finely carried on. It is for consumptives, and only hopeful cases are admitted. Another hospital, called 'St. Catherine's Home,' admits advanced cases. It is a delightful spot for the poor sufferers.

"Well, I have told you of Ventnor, but can not begin to describe half of the wonderful and beautiful sights that meet my eye at every turn. Our holiday is nearly ended, and we go back to London very soon. Ventnor is the queen of towns, for its interest and picturesqueness; it will linger in my memory for many years as a pleasant dream. The little donkey, that draws the water from the well in Carisbrook Castle, is very cunning and deserves mention."

Pearl wrote: "*My Dearest Home Folks,—* You see, we are now in London, and I will say that we have not seen a glimpse of the sun since leaving lovely Ventnor. The snow-storm has entirely disappeared, but it is so miserable; fog and mud abound everywhere. However, we are having a fine time. We all went to the French Hippodrome; we could not get seats, so had a box, next to the royal box. The performance was magnificent. We were so excited during the 'Stag Hunt,' that I nearly fell over the side of the box. The hunt began with the huntsmen coming in and sounding a bugle, calling the people to the 'Meet.' They came in, dressed in red hunting suits; ladies in red habits. A pack of hounds came in baying, and at a given signal, off they went, with the ladies and gentlemen after them. Then the stag comes bounding in, pursued by the hounds and hunters. I wish you could have seen the horses jump ditches, walls, and fences. One horse went over a table with dishes and glasses on it, and did not make them even rattle. Then they came home, after killing the stag, or appearing to do so, and danced by moonlight on the green.

"After it was over we went through the stables, saw the beautiful creatures, and patted them. I was invited to sing at a concert given at the Bunhill Fields' Mission Rooms. The people who go there are all poor, picked out of the slums of London. The hall was packed, and they all looked so poor and distressed. During the first of the programme there was not much enthusiasm, but when it was announced that a lady from America would sing, they began to clap furiously. I could not sing any thing light, for as I looked at them my heart went out in pity for their poverty. So I began:

> " ' There were ninety-and-nine, that safely lay
>   In the shelter of the fold,
>   But one was out on the hills away,
>   Far off from the gates of gold.'

"As I went on, an intense hush came; you could have hard a pin drop; when I ended, with 'Rejoice! for the Lord brings back his own,' there was the wildest burst of applause, which could hardly be stopped. It touched their hearts, the story of the Saviour's love. I had been longing to give some hope and comfort to these wretched people, and felt rejoiced that I could do so, even in the smallest degree.

"We went again to Madame Tussaud's, and had the honor to sit in the carriage of the great Napoleon, which was used on his journey to Moscow. Then we went down into the 'Chamber of Horrors.' It was frightful, and I would n't go again for a mint of money. Figures of people of the most horrible description; a scaffold, and beside it a wretched old man awaiting death. We came out as soon as possible, fairly frightened, but laughed when we thought we had been afraid of wax figures.

"We are making plans to leave London for Germany, in April, and have written to secure a boarding-place, which has been highly spoken of to us. We have received an invitation to spend a month with a lovely English family, who live out of London. We shall accept and consider ourselves very fortunate.

"Frances and I went down to the United States' Legation to get our passports, for we must have them in Germany. We had a letter to the secretary, from the bankers, Baring Bros., so asked for him. Much to our surprise he was quite a young man, but very polite and kind. We had to swear allegiance to the United States, and then he took a description of us. It was rather embarrassing when he mentioned color of my eyes, smallness of my mouth, and fairness of complexion. Frances had to be put down as slight, blue eyes, sandy hair, and fair complexion. But we obtained the passports, paying one guinea apiece.

" I have just received this letter in answer to the one I sent to Germany. I will give a literal translation of it :

"'BERLIN, 20th.

"'21 KONIGIN-AUGUSTA STRASSE.

"' *Most Honored Fraulein,*—Your letter from London have I received, and would myself much joy give, you in April as members of my family, in my house to see. I can to you a very comfortable home-like front room give, in which a piano a place could find. The monthly price, including board, light, service, and fire, will amount to 130 marks [a mark is 25 cents]. The city of Berlin is very beautiful in the spring ; we have much good music, and our house is directly on the Zoological Gardens, so that we many beautiful walks together can take. Your home-sickness will quickly vanish, when you first your studies with Professor R—— begin, and yourself much with German language occupy, which in our family always spoken is. You will be very kind, if you me will soon let know if you are coming April 1st, so that I the room reserve can, that at present is occupied by an American. In the hope you soon to know and to greet, am I,

"' Yours forever,   LOUISE V——.'

"Now do n't you think that is a pretty letter? We are delighted with the prospect of a nice home, in a congenial family. Hurrah for Germany! With love,   PEARL."

XI.

ACROSS THE ENGLISH CHANNEL.

"BERLIN, GERMANY, April —.

"*My Dear Mother :*

HOW strange it seems to write the above, but so it is, and we are now in the city of Berlin. We are American or English no longer, but true '*Deutschy.*' When I say that, Frances remarks, 'My dear Pearl, *we* are always *American girls*, under all circumstances.' That is true, and we are very proud of the fact.

"Taking the train from London, after parting with our dear friends with sorrow, we went to Queensboro'; there boarded a steamer, taking berths in the second-class cabin, and settled ourselves for repose.

"False delusion! As the ticket-man had said, it bid fair to be a nasty night. His words proved true; not only true, but twice, thrice, true. Rough? Well, rather! Pitch? I should say so! I was not seasick, but poor

Frances was the picture of despair. We had a fearful passage over, and sleep was impossible.

"We landed in Flushing, Holland, at 6:45 A. M., and such a dismal-looking crowd as got off that boat, — it was really laughable! Frances could hardly walk, but managed to reach the train, which was in waiting. In the same carriage were three English girls and two German men. One of the girls remembered seeing us at Ventnor. The carriages were very comfortable, and we had a nice sleep. We were awakened by the guards at the station, and hot beef-tea was handed in, which was very refreshing.

" When our baggage was to be inspected, we all had to leave the train and go into a large room, but should have fared badly, as we could not understand a word the officials said, had not the young German in our carriage come to the rescue and shouted, *Nein ! nein !* meaning that our baggage was not dutiable.

"We had only one change more on our journey to Berlin. It was a long, tedious journey. At the stations it was fun to see the officials in blue suits and red caps, talking so fast in German. In the fields women were digging and drawing carts; sometimes a woman would be yoked with a cow, drawing a cart. We had plenty of fruit to eat, and hot cups of coffee were also handed in at the stations; then on the train would go, and the guard would take the cups.

"We reached Hanover at 6 P. M.; it is a fine city. Then past a magnificent range of mountains and a beautiful lake. Berlin was reached at 11 P. M. We were so glad to come to the end of our journey, and rejoiced to see the kindly face of Fraulein V——, who spoke to us at once. We were so tired that we slept until two o'clock the next afternoon.

"This house is a *pension*, and we are three flights up. It is on the corner of two streets, and the view is fine, looking out on Konigin-Augusta Strasse, one of the finest streets in Berlin. It is very wide, and in the middle, boats or barges are constantly going up and down the broad canal, which is lined on either side with trees. Very near us is a large square, where five streets meet, and horse-cars, stages, and people congregate at this point. All the buildings are handsome and look so clean,—very different from London.

"Our room is nice. In one corner of it is a queer stove, snow-white, reaching nearly to the ceiling and handsomely carved. We have a very nice table, not at all German as yet.

" It is charming weather, quite warm, and the sky is so blue and clear. The German officers are seen everywhere, and are fine-looking. Do n't worry about us, for we shall prosper in German land. With love, PEARL."

The time slipped away, and the girls improved it by studying hard. They had a fine teacher in German, and were now able to converse fairly well. Their previous study helped them, but contact with people who spoke the language was a great advantage. During this pleasant season they made little trips to points of interest. Going to Charlottenburg, a suburb of Berlin, they saw the palace, built of yellow stone and guarded by soldiers.

In the palace garden is the mausoleum where the late kaiser's father and mother are buried. The floor is beautifully inlaid, and the life-size, recumbent statues of the king and queen are side by side. Looking down upon them is a picture of the Saviour, and over all is thrown a bright blue light, from glass in the roof. The effect upon the marble is exquisite. The gardens are beautiful,—a wilderness of flowers.

As they came through the town, a fair or

market was being held in the middle of the street, and the peasants, in a variety of costumes were selling every thing, from a wash-tub to a pair of boots, and having such a good time.

Potsdam is half an hour's journey from Berlin. When they arrived there the first thing their eyes fell upon was a large red sign, stating that there was the "place for Americans to have their photographs taken for ten cents, in two minutes and a quarter, with frame, and a hook at the end, to hang it up by," as Dickens says. They entered and astonished the proprietor at the number of persons he must put in one small picture. The result was a curiosity, which being sent home, served to make sport for the family and friends.

After leaving the "American artist," they turned their steps to the Winter palace of Frederick the Great. As they entered the courtyard, past marching sentinels, a clatter of wheels was heard, and two coal-black horses, drawing the carriage of Prince Leopold, came in sight. They caught a glimpse of the prince as he went by. They were shown through the palace by a guide, who seeing they were Americans, spoke in English, talking about "Fredericks the Greats," much to their amusement.

Then they went to the Sans Souci Palace gardens, which are very lovely. There they ate a lunch in the open air; another party of Americans, red guide books in hand, were met, and they all marched in solemn procession through the palace. On coming out, as Pearl said, "suddenly we heard an explosion; the cause was a bottle of seltzer water in my bag; the cork had flown away, making a terrific noise. I shudder to think of the consequences if it had occurred in the palace."

Next they went through a beautiful park, to the new palace, where the late crown prince, Emperor Frederick, lived in summer. It was magnificent; one room was made of shells and precious stones. Taking a carriage, they drove to the kaiser's summer palace, built in Gothic style, on a high hill, sloping down to a lovely lake. The private rooms of the kaiser are very simple; a little iron bed, covered with a gray army blanket, and light wood furniture. In the gardens they were attacked by an army of wasps. As Frances wrote, "They probably knew we were not of royal birth, and were not good enough to sting, so we escaped injury. I wish they could have known we were *royal Americans.*"

MOUNTAIN VIEW IN GERMANY.

They had now a delightful circle of friends, both Americans and Germans. The latter were so friendly, simple, and unreserved in their manners, and the girls were made welcome guests among them. Pearl wrote home a glowing account of their attending a "Commers."

"Now I do n't suppose you have any idea what a 'Commers' is? Well, it is a gathering of all the German students in a great hall, where speeches are made, and they sing their college-songs. We went with a party of young Americans and had a very nice time. We were most honored guests, I can assure you, were given seats in the gallery, and cake, coffee, and candy were sent to us.

"This is what we saw: an enormous hall, trimmed with flowers and flags of all the different societies of the college. Four hundred students, all in costume, seated at long tables, two officers in full uniform at each table. At a given signal from the president, these men rose, and such a chorus of melody as burst forth! Speeches were made, and a sword drill given. One of the officers made a fine speech to the ladies, who had honored them by their presence, he alluded to America; and he sat down covered with applause and confusion, for the students made the hall ring with their shouts. Then the president greeted us in splendid English. Every thing was done for our pleasure, and we think German students very polite.

"Now I must tell you of a social party we attended. It began at seven o'clock, with a German play in three acts, which was finely done. We could understand the German quite well. After the play, a fine supper. The company were Germans, English, and Americans. One young man said, 'I should think you were from Boston.' I said, 'I have that honor.' He said he knew by the way I talked, so different from a New-Yorker or a Westerner.

"There was a Roumanian prince at the party, but I begged not to be introduced, as I could n't speak Italian, and he could n't speak English. The party was a grand affair.

"We attend the American Church, and it seems so homelike to have an American minister and congregation. Sunday evenings he receives at his own house, and gives a lecture on some interesting topic. It is of very great advantage to students in the city to have such an influence for good about them, and all are welcome to this hospitable home. An effort will be made, in fact has been, to build a suitable church edifice here in Berlin."

A fine concert was given at the Zoological Gardens. The scene was enchanting; the grounds were lighted by electricity, and trimmed with flags and lanterns. Two fine orchestras charmed the immense throng of people with delightful music. At intervals a roar or a howl from some lion or tiger would be heard, which lent a variety to the programme. The feeding of the animals was a curious but a terrible sight. The eagles would swoop down, seize a piece of meat, and then fly to the top of a monstrous cage. The lions and tigers were kept in outside cages, but were fed in the inside cages. At a given signal all the doors opened, and out they would come with a rush, wild with hunger. A tremendous howling and bounding against the sides of the cages followed until the keeper had thrown them their meal of raw meat. Frances said she would rather be excused from meeting one of them, especially if it happened to be hungry.

They visited the art museums, and found a fine collection of casts. As Pearl wrote, "Frances is very enthusiastic over the old masters. I must confess that I enjoy the modern paintings much more. I suppose it shows poor taste. Give me a piece of music, and I can tell its beauty at once, but the old masters I will leave for my Sister Frances to describe. We are now planning to leave Berlin, for August, but have not decided yet where we may go. We wish to find some quiet, out-of-the-way place, and see a little of German country life."

The time had passed very rapidly away since they first came to Berlin. As they had studied very hard for a long time, a rest was needed.

"LAASE, ISLAND OF RÜGEN, GERMANY,

"*Aug.* ——

"*Beloved Home Circle:* Little did I ever think that one day I should write you a letter from Rügen. We are here in a spot that until three weeks ago we hardly knew existed, or at least did not realize the fact. We heard of this place through Frau V——, and the family where we are staying are her cousins.

"Well, we started at five o'clock in the morning, and took the train to Stralsund. It was a pretty journey, through a farming country, along fields of grain, with lovely corn flowers and poppies scattered over the fields, and reached Stralsund at 12:30. It is such a queer, old German town, quite famous, being the only one that Wallenstein, in the thirty years' war, failed to capture. He said 'he would have it, though it were chained to Heaven.'

"At the station we engaged a porter to take our baggage to the boat. So he put the trunks into a little blue hand-cart, and started off, we trudging on behind. It really was the most primitive thing, and we were objects of curiosity to the inhabitants of the place. After seeing our baggage in the steamer *Hertha*, off we went again to view the sights, visiting two beautiful churches, the quaint museum, and town hall. I could almost imagine I had stepped back into mediæval times, every thing looked so ancient.

"After dinner at Hotel Bismarck, we waited until three o'clock, then set sail for Rügen. I can not describe the loveliness of that sail on the Baltic. It was a charming day, not at all rough, and we enjoyed the three hours' sail very much. At a little after six o'clock, we came to the landing-stage Vieregge. Out came a sail-boat to take us to land, and away went the *Hertha*, with the adieus of our fellow-passengers floating over the water.

"In a few moments we arrived, and were met by the friends with whom we are now staying. A span of good horses soon took us across the country to Laase.

"How can I give you any idea of this place and household? It is an ideal German farmer's family; good-hearted, simple-minded, and impressed with the idea that America is a heathen country. They can not speak English, and we try to speak our very best German. It is very amusing, and we surprise them by telling great stories of our noble land.

"The family consists of the old father, who

LUCIA.

sits in his corner and smokes a pipe reaching to the floor; the mother, who is a personified German dame; a daughter, a rosy-cheeked lassie, ready to do the honors of the place, by taking us to drive and to walk; also a son, who is in the army, but home on a vacation, very gallant and gay. The house is of stone, and the barn-yard is directly opposite, with three big barns — thatched roofs — looking very picturesque. As for live stock, I am sure you would say it was a Noah's ark. They have thirty horses, thirty cows, four hundred sheep, a dozen cats, twenty dogs, thirty pigs, hens and chickens by the hundred, geese and ducks, which waddle along in stately procession, quacking all the time, doves that bill and coo about four o'clock every morning, when one would far rather sleep than listen to the cooing of doves.

"We go to ride in the hay-cart, and bounce up and down the hills. In fact, we have thrown all care to the winds, and are now country lassies. This is a wheat farm of six or seven hundred acres, and now they are harvesting the grain. As we look off for miles, we can see the yellow grain stacked up in sheaves.

"The other morning, came one of the maidens who harvest the grain, and bound upon our arms a band of wheat, tied with blue ribbon. She sang a little German ditty very sweetly. It is a pretty custom, and we gave her a piece of money.

"We are resting and enjoying country-life

The garden is beautiful, and we sit out of doors, sometimes reading, but looking with untiring eyes at the scene spread before us. Being on an arm of the Baltic sea we can enjoy the sea air as well as the country air, and the water view is superb. We are a mile from a village of thirty little houses, all with straw roofs.

"We called on an old aunt of Frau V——, who lives in this village. She was a genuine old-country woman, so pleasant and very glad to see us. She gave us a glass of raspberry shrub, in the most hospitable manner. Then we called on the village pastor, and Sunday went to the little stone church, which looks so very ancient. We could n't quite understand all of the service, but it was a touching sight to see the white-haired pastor, in cap and gown, stand up to address his little flock. Truly, I feel as if I was in another world, and I am tempted to cry, 'Can this be I?'

"We shall not remain here the whole month, but go to other parts of the island; visit the larger towns, and make excursions on the sea. We have company here to-day, who have come to see the wonder. American girls are as much of a curiosity as a Turk would be in some small New Hampshire village,

ALONG THE RHINE.

"I could never cease writing of the delights and the loveliness of this beautiful island, but will continue later.

"With love,   FRANCES."

So the lovely summer days flew by, each one being marked by some new delight. The strangers were made much of, and invited to the homes of the good people. One afternoon they rode in the hay-cart, drawn by four horses, into the fields, and there remained for hours watching the men and women at work. They ran races, and Pearl gained courage to mount the raking machine, and guide the old horse, who would not go out of a walk, although urged to do so by the son Otto. Then they come home in the gloaming, tired but happy.

Their German was improving, as they were obliged to talk in that language to all the people about them. They were great favorites in the family. As Pearl wrote, "One of the fine horses has been named 'America,' and another 'Boston,' in honor of *us* and of our dear country. But I do love Germany better than I ever thought possible. Frances frowns when I rave over this foreign country, but I know she is as much charmed as I am."

A trip around the island had been planned; so early one lovely morning, their friends arranged to drive them to Putbus, a distance of fifteen miles. Otto and Lucia went with them, and a jolly time they had. The way led past wheat fields, funny little villages, where dogs, hens, and white-headed children abounded, who stared at the strangers open-mouthed, as they drove along. Bergen, the capital of the island of Rügen, was reached, and they ascended the tower, erected to the memory of the Poet Andt. They inscribed their names in the " strangers' book," and then went on to Putbus. They went to Bellevue hotel, where they were to meet a party of friends, who welcomed them heartily. Otto and Lucia spent the whole day with them, but as evening came on, they parted from these kind people with regret.

The next morning it was raining, but donning water-proofs, they set out to points of interest. A fine park, in which is the palace of the mother of the Prince of Putbus, was first seen. Walking one and a half miles, the little place of Lauterbach, which is located directly on the open sea, was reached. Returning to dinner at Putbus, they rested and then set out to view the wonders.

Putbus is a fascinating place, and is the residence of the Prince of Putbus, who has a magnificent palace in the center of a large deer park. There is also a college, which is attended by two hundred students. They visited the palace, and were fortunate enough to see the prince at one of the windows.

Early the next morning they drove to Binz, a bathing resort. On the way, the hunting castle of the prince was seen. It is built in the midst of a dense forest; a winding road leads up and up to the top; suddenly the gray stone castle bursts upon the view. The view from the tower was glorious. The ocean, pretty white cottages, wheat fields, and for miles around the dense forest were visible. They could hardly bear to leave it, but hunger called, and they they must stop for dinner at Binz. The afternoon was spent walking on the beach and in the woods, sitting on the rocks, breathing in the sea air, as Pearl said, "just being lazy." At seven o'clock a row-boat took them to the steamer, that was to go to Sassnitz, where they arrived after a rough passage, about nine o'clock. It was too late to do any thing but go to a hotel, where the strangers were kindly treated.

The next day they found a nice room in a

private villa, where they could keep house on a small scale. Their friends obtained rooms in the same villa, and this made it very pleasant for all. How charming it was, taking breakfast and tea on the balcony, looking off on the sea and watching the ships, also the people on the pier below; then having a nice dinner at the hotel, where the circle of Germans, English, and Americans made it seem like home, for good will and a friendly feeling prevailed.

Pearl wrote, " As far as people go Sassnitz is a regular watering-place, being very popular, but for walks and scenery it is superb. Look where you will there is beauty. In front the boundless sea, and at the back the dense forests. One usually finds woods without water, or water without woods, but here both are combined.

" There are many excursions to be taken from here. One of the most delightful we enjoyed a few days ago, when the sea was calm. After dinner we took the steamer *Rügen* and sailed to the light-house of Acona. The steamer was crowded with people, as the day was superb. We sailed along past the wonderful cliffs of Stubbenkammer and Lohme for two hours, and feasted our eyes on the magnificent scenery. We remained two hours at Acona and then set sail for Sassnitz.

"It was so beautiful coming back, as we saw the sunset on the sea, and the darkness stealing over all this beauty; after which they lit the cliffs from the ship with electric lights. It was like fairy land. Imagine a great chalk cliff, or rather many of them, rising out of the sea, amidst a dense forest, which comes down to within six feet of the ocean; then the glowing light over all, which at times would be thrown on the sail-boats going by, making them look like white wings. I thought of angels near us, keeping watch over mortals. I can never forget that lovely trip. Frances kept very quiet, but I could see by her eyes, that all this loveliness was being stored away, and that some day she would weave it together in a fascinating way.

"Then our party arranged to visit Stubben-kammer, which is a distance of seven and a half miles. It was proposed for us to walk, but at last only three were willing to try that plan, the others going another way in the post-wagon.

"So Frances and I, with an escort, started on our trip. We were rejoiced at the decision, and enjoyed our tramp exceedingly. The way led through woods, a nice shady path, up hill and down, with little brooks at times running across our path; then we would come to an open space, where the sea in all its glory would burst upon our view. We arrived at twelve o'clock, not very much tired, but glad to rest on the rocks after dinner.

"Then we went out in a sail-boat to the cliffs and mounted them. They are perfectly wonderful. The three principal ones are, The Konigs Stuhl, Victoria Sicht, and King Wilhelm's Sicht. Frances said if we had such a spot in America, it would be spoilt in a few years by hotels and tourists. Here it is all so simple and natural, which is the great charm of the place. The ordinary American traveller never comes to this spot, and I do n't think there are more than ten or twelve Americans here.

"In the afternoon we walked to a beautiful fresh-water lake, in the midst of a dense wood. One would think that the ocean was miles away, but it was only ten minutes' walk. We all came home in the post-wagon, very tired, but more than satisfied with our delightful trip."

So every day was marked by some great

pleasure. The girls were gaining strength for the winter's work, and storing their minds with knowledge of the world, outside their own country.

> "HOTEL D'ANGLETERRE, COPENHAGUE,
> "*Aug. 27th.*

"*My Dearest Family*,— I can almost see the look of astonishment, and hear the exclamations that will arise, as this letter is received. Mamma will think we are at the world's end, and have grave doubts as to our ever returning. Truly, dear people, if any one had told us a week ago, that we should take a trip to the moon, we should have believed it quite as much as being told we should visit Copenhagen, Denmark.

"This is how it happened: Our friends wished to join an excursion to come here, and as it was very cheap, I decided to seize the opportunity, and Pearl was wild with delight at the prospect, so we joined the party, as we could not resist the temptation. Now I shall describe the journey as well as I can.

"At 9:30 P. M. we saw the lights of the steamer coming from Stettin to take her Sassnitz passengers. At a given signal we put out in small boats, leaving the pier crowded with spectators; reached the steamer safely, and at once procured berths in the ladies' cabin; then went to bed, and as the passage was good, to sleep.

"About five o'clock in the morning the fog-horn began to blow; a heavy fog had arisen, and the captain did not dare to go on, for we were in the harbor, surrounded by shipping. We waited, and then the fog began to lift; the sun was fighting its way through the mass of fog, spreading a rosy glow over the water and several sail-boats, making the scene wonderful in the extreme.

"At 8 A. M. we arrived in Copenhagen and walked to the Hotel d'Angleterre, breakfasted, and then started out to see the sights. We walked through many streets, went to the market, where the funny old women, in queer gowns and sun-bonnets, were crying their wares. We found that these people knew we were Americans, and always answered us in broken English. We can not disguise our nationality, even if we speak in our best German or French.

"We walked to the famous Christianborg Palace, which was nearly destroyed by fire. The grand structure must have been colossal.

COPENHAGEN.

Then went to the Ethnographical Museum, where a fine collection of curiosities from Greenland, North America, and China represent the way the people of those different countries live. Leaving the museum, the way led through a fine park to Rosenberg Palace, built by Christian II, and filled with every thing beautiful. We joined a party just going in, and a dapper young man guided us through. As his auditors were Germans, English, and Danish, he tried to please all by speaking those languages. The palace was magnificent, with rooms of a very early date, coming to a more modern period, while at the last our own time was shown, with the most costly and elegant belongings. We were so tired after viewing all this splendor that we rested until the next morning.

"The next day we set sail bright and early for Helingor, a seaport town, two hours from Copenhagen. The coast was very pretty all the way, passing little watering-places and small towns. Then on to Helinborg in Sweden, only divided from Denmark by a strait. We laughed to think we were on the soil of Sweden, and roamed about the quaint old town, going back to the steamer for dinner.

"Coming up the harbor of Copenhagen, it was noticed that all the vessels were decorated with flags, and a great stir being made. On inquiry, were told that the Emperor and Empress of Russia had come to visit the King of Denmark. The whole city was in an uproar. Every street decorated, and grand celebrations everywhere. That evening we spent in Tivoli Garden, where festivities were held. The Danes were out in full glory of dress, in pretty costumes of red and blue, embroidered in bright colors. A building to represent 'Aladdin's Palace,' with towers and domes, lit by colored lights; a pantomime; a dazzling illumination of the gardens, and fireworks were some of the wonders displayed. Pearl said, 'Are we in the land of the living, or Wonderland?' We could hardly tell that night, but came back to earth by breakfast time next morning.

"We spent some time in the Royal Picture Gallery, where the modern artists are better represented than the old masters, although they have a few gems. The collection of antiquities was very interesting; it began with the flint age, then bronze, iron, gold, silver, and wood were represented. It was curious to note the progress of man from the earliest ages, and see how he improved, as time went on.

"The next morning we had not walked very far after leaving our hotel before we heard a great noise in the street. Word was given that the emperor and empress would ride from church that way. A sound of music told us that royalty was approaching. We were rewarded by seeing them, and the empress bowed very sweetly as she passed by. Several other carriages were in the procession, containing royalty, but we did not know who they were.

"A visit to Thorwaldsen's Museum of Statuary was next in order. In fact, to see this was the principal reason of our coming here. It is noted throughout the world for its beauty, and well it may be. I only wish I could afford to bring home models of a *few* of the finest, but must be content to see the originals. Thorwaldsen's grave is in the middle of the museum, and he sleeps there, surrounded by his precious statues. We roamed through the beautiful rooms, feasting our eyes on the exquisite loveliness around us. Mercury, Venus, Jason, Psyche, Ganymede, are some of the finest, but no pen of mine can do justice to them. All I can say is, that they are the grandest specimens of art.

"The steamer which will take us to Sassnitz will start to-morrow, and if all goes well we shall go to Berlin in a few days. This will end a most delightful vacation, and we return in good health and spirits. Pearl looks hardly like the same girl, her cheeks are so rosy, and she is as brown as a berry. I will leave Pearl to describe my general appearance, but think I have gained very much in strength of body, and I hope of mind also.

"With love,   FRANCES."

Frances and Pearl had now to make their plans for the coming winter in Berlin. It was decided to change their place of abode, and go into a real German family, where that language was always spoken; for Frau V—— had so many Americans in her family, it was a great temptation to speak English.

They were now up four flights of stairs, but as Pearl said, "We are used to mounting stairs by this time." The view from their room was lovely, as it faced a large square, adorned with trees and fountains; while beyond the whole length of Bulow Strasse, for nearly two miles, could be seen. The room was very pretty with its Turkish rug, large center-table, easy chairs, a bed-lounge, olive green and red rep, cream lace draperies, long pier-glass, and a fine piano. These, with their books, pictures, and many ornaments, made up a lovely home-like spot for them to enjoy, and they were much delighted with their surroundings.

Study was now the order of the day, but many social pleasures were enjoyed. Pearl was working very hard, and Herr Professor seemed much satisfied. One day, however, after she had sung a selection, he said, "You sing flat." She again tried the strain, and he said the same, but at last she succeeded in pleasing him. So with the next pupil, and also the next one, the same complaint. At last he screamed, "All my pupils are flats." As Pearl said, "He meant we all sang flat," but a hearty laugh followed this remark. I said, 'Oh! Herr Professor, do not scold us too hard, for the day is so very damp, it makes one sing badly.' He began to look more pleasant, and at last was as jolly as ever."

A social club had been formed, the object of which was to read German, and each contribute to the pleasure of the members by singing or reading, and essays were given on different subjects of interest.

One evening the club met with a German family, and the host very politely gave Pearl a bunch of lily-of-the-valley, saying, " I gif zie flower to zie flower." She was very much pleased, and thanked him, in her best German, for the pretty compliment.

At the time of their sojourn in Berlin, the Emperor William I, or the old kaiser, was alive and able to go about. Attending the opera one evening, they saw the kaiser, a noble-looking man, who was there with his favorite daughter, the Grand Duchess of Baden. He was worshipped by his subjects, for the Germans are a very loyal people. In the Kaiser's Museum were seen a wonderful collection of quaint carvings and beautiful china; also the gifts given to the kaiser on his birthday; they were of gold and silver, and also a large clock covered with jewels. As Frances wrote, "After leaving the museum we happened to think that we might see the kaiser in his palace, so we started, and were walking along leisurely, when we heard the music of the guard, who salute him every day. We ran just as fast as we could, and succeeded in reaching the place as the kaiser made his appearance at the windows, smiling and bowing to the host of people, who swung their hats and handkerchiefs in the air and cheered with a right good will. Dear, old man, his subjects were loyal to the last!

"We walk in the wonderful Thiergarten every pleasant day. One can hardly form an idea of its beauty, until seen in reality. It extends twelve miles, a perfect labyrinth of trees, flowers, fountains, and lovely statuary. One can walk for hours, and see something new and interesting every moment. Going down one shady path, at the end of it you will find another still more beautiful, with a gleaming piece of marble shining through the trees. You think, 'I must see that,' and then behold something else in the distance, from which you can not turn away, and so on from one beautiful object to another.

"Fraulein Loisinger, a prima donna from Darmstadt, is boarding with us. She is very jolly, and as she can not speak English, we have to converse in German entirely, which is of advantage to us. She is a pleasant companion and walks with us in the Thiergarten."

The girls, with the assistance of Frau S——, gave an afternoon reception to several of their young lady friends. The door was opened into an adjoining room, which made it charming;

coffee and little cakes were served at five o'clock. Then each one gave a song, or a sonata by Beethoven, or read a poem, making it a lovely little affair.

"If we do our very best to make others happy, we enjoy ourselves all the more," Frances said.

"We have had a most exciting time this week. Professor G—— arrived unexpectedly with a party of five boys, whom he is taking through Europe. They remained only three days, but those days will be long remembered in this pension. They were all between seventeen and twenty years old, but so full of life and fun that poor Professor G—— was in despair. I think in those three days they saw the whole of Berlin, and every thing 'seeable' in it. However, they were such nice, genuine Yankee lads, that even when they talked about being 'sold,' and other similar expressions, it sounded like music to our ears, —so like our dear boys at home!

"We left them alone at supper one night, when we went to Wansea, and they said that Dick, John, and Frank ate all the supper, and Charlie and Harry finished the dishes, which was nearly true.

BEETHOVEN'S HOME.

"Oh! that lovely trip to Wansea, on a beautiful October afternoon. This place is situated on a charming lake. We walked about for awhile, and then took a boat and went out upon the lake, to watch the sunset. Never have I seen such a glorious sight; the clouds were wonderful, and all was so quiet, it seemed like looking into Heaven. We did not say a word, a laugh was not heard, we sat perfectly quiet; the good Dr. T—— put down the oars, and the only sound heard was the singing of the birds and a strain of distant music. It made me homesick for the first time since coming to Berlin, and you all, dear home people, were in my thoughts. At last the glorious orb departed to America, said Dr. T——, and the spell was broken; we came back to earth. That memory will never leave me.

"We are to attend the Philharmonic concerts; the first one was a Beethoven evening. Joachim played four times, and such applause I never heard. After he had finished playing, he was crowned with a laurel wreath, and it seemed as if the people would go wild with excitement. We are to have a real Thanksgiving festival, and a dinner which will make us think of our own dear country. It is to be given by the American Church, and we are to work for its success. We shall think of the dear home circle on that day."

XII.

HOLIDAYS IN GERMANY.

THE Sunday before Thanksgiving Day these words fell on the ears of the people who had came to praise God for all his mercies. The good pastor of the American Church in Berlin began his sermon to his loved flock, who were nearly all strangers in this foreign land, saying:

"Our honored president, in his proclamation appointing November 24th as a day for thanksgiving, says: 'Let families and kindred be united on that day, and let their hearts, filled with kindly cheer, be turned in thankfulness to the Source of all their pleasures, and the Giver of all that makes the day glad and joyous.'"

Ah! how few who listened to this message would be with the home-circle on that day! Only in thought could they be united. But kindly hearts and willing hands are to be found everywhere, and the good ladies of this church were preparing an "American Home Gathering." The invitations given made many Americans wonder what was in store for them, for the evening of Nov. 24th.

Frances and Pearl entered heart and soul into this festival, lending a helping hand wherever it was needed. A fine musical programme had been arranged, and Pearl was to lend her voice for the occasion. Frances said, "I can not sing, but I can think, and I have helped dear papa so many times to arrange for festivals that I can suggest the best and easiest way to arrange for such an occasion."

The day dawned bright and clear, and was spent by the ladies in giving the finishing touches to their work. As the hour arrived, about two hundred and fifty persons, representing not only American but several other nations, met in the Architektenhaus, a large hall, between six and seven o'clock. The room was filled with tables, at each of which eight persons could be seated.

At a given signal parties were formed, and all were in their places at the tables, with happy faces, eager to hear what Dr. S—— would say in his "Address of Welcome." It was a true welcome all through, and his closing words: "American hearts, American homes — God bless them all," were echoed, if not audibly, in the hearts of all present.

A blessing was asked, and then came the supper,—a bounteous fare, with real American cooking, of turkey, mince-pie, and plum-pudding. Judging from the happiness displayed in the faces, many wished to say, "God bless the Ladies' Union." The result showed that they had all worked in perfect union.

After the supper was ended, the musical programme was finely given. Piano solos, songs, and a violin solo, were listened to with great pleasure. Then a quartette was announced; the name was not given, but all were asked to join in the chorus. When "The Star-spangled Banner" was begun, how the hundreds of voices took up the strain, so familiar to all "The Star-spangled Banner, long may it wave," until it seemed as if the echo must reach to the very shores of "the Land of the Free, and the Home of the Brave."

Then the young people played American games, laughing and talking, in joyousness of youth. As the evening waned, college songs were sung, and "Home, Sweet Home," was given, but at the last the company joined in "My Country, 't is of Thee," and with a handshake and a good-bye, this grand festival was over.

Frances in writing home said, "I felt as if we were among the favored of earth; but it seemed as if you all must be there, and that you must hear and know what we were enjoying. I felt happy, yet sad, and when we sang 'My Country,' I could not finish, but laid my head down on the table and had a good cry. I was not alone, for many shed tears. I think they must have been tears of joy for our many blessings. I often think of what dear Kitty Lee used to say, 'Do n't be serious, girls'; so I will change the subject and tell you of a birthday party, where we had a very *lively* time. It was the birthday of Herr Rosenberger, and fifteen guests were invited to celebrate it.

"A German birthday party is a very queer thing; the gentlemen always embrace the host, and it seems so funny to see them hugging each other. Then such a dinner! We sat down at 8:30 P. M., and rose from the table at 10:30 P. M. It was a fine spread, arranged in German style.

"We returned to the parlor, and a maid servant, in lieu of finger bowls, brought an atomizer, with which the face was sprinkled, and poured ointment on the hands. The perfume was delicious and very lasting. Of course we had to converse in German all the evening. We were complimented on our improvement, and Dr. T—— said he should not dare to correct us now, as he did when we first came to Germany.

" Pearl was asked to sing, and he exclaimed in his very best English, ' And the song from beginning to end, I found again in the heart of a friend.' This was a very pretty compliment to her musical ability, the remembrance of that song which had so lingered in his memory. Oh! the kindly German people, so simple in their ways, yet so intelligent.

"The guests brought as gifts lovely flowers and little pot-plants full of blossoms, wishing the host many returns of the day.

"There are a great many Jews in Berlin, and we are quite used to seeing them in the streets. We went with dear Mrs. L——, who is taking such good care of us, to the Jewish synagogue. The service was very interesting, although it seemed queer to us. The men sit downstairs, and the women upstairs. The priest, dressed in a purple gown and cap, sings the service, with trills and many runs up and down the scale, while the people sit still and listen. It was very curious, and we were glad to add to our knowledge of their manners and customs."

Pearl wrote, "I think I ought to send you a few words once in awhile, and I will describe a lovely wedding to which we were bidden; for I know it will interest all the girls. The youngest daughter of my dear old professor was married to another professor. The ceremony was in church, and the altar was beautifully trimmed with flowers. The happy pair came in together, and sat down in two chairs in front of the minister. They were followed by *twelve* bridesmaids dressed in pink, white, and blue, who also sat around the couple in a circle. Then came Prof. S——, his wife, and all the guests in full dress. It was the first wedding I ever attended where singing was an attraction, and such singing—perfectly grand! A choir composed of the first artists in Berlin gave this delightful music.

"The bride, a lovely girl, wore a white satin dress, with a veil, and looked like all brides, whether in America or Germany; the only difference in her attire being that she wore myrtle instead of orange blossoms. The bridegroom was a noble-looking man, and all seemed very happy.

"It was a sweet pretty wedding. Frances said it made her think of her girls, and the many times they had gone as unbidden guests to a church wedding, to see the lovely bride and wonder how it must all seem, to be so beautiful and so beloved. It was our first German wedding, and we much enjoyed the treat.

"The weather is now becoming colder, and we shall soon wrap ourselves up in our new fur cloaks and thick flannels. We are having some thick woolen dresses made, for in this climate one needs the very warmest clothing. But it seems to agree with us nicely, and I feel so strong and able to work hard. Frances is really gaining in flesh, and her 'lily white' cheeks are quite rosy, especially after a long walk in the bracing air.

"Christmas is rapidly approaching, and the whole city of Berlin is being turned into a big market or store. The streets are filled with booths, which are trimmed with Christmas wreaths and evergreen, surrounded by Christmas trees of all sizes. The peasants have come in, bringing their own handiwork, and call their wares from morning until late at night.

"The shops are filled with every thing rich and rare, and all the streets are ablaze with light when evening comes. We gaze in rapture, but keep tight hold of our pocket-books, until we can decide what to buy with our Christmas money, which dear papa and mamma sent in such good season.

"However, we have been promised a real German Christmas tree, therefore feel quite excited over the prospect. It is to be kept a secret, and we are not even to guess, until Christmas Eve, what is being done for our pleasure. But we have a plan to return the surprise to our kind friends.

"We are now studying hard, for a vacation will be given during the Christmas holidays. We are both much occupied with our different studies. Frances has literature, German, and French, which with her daily writing, keeps her very busy. My music, both vocal and instrumental, also German and French, hardly give me a moment of leisure. We study through the day, but rest evenings, so thus keep our health and strength.

"A lovely American lady, who is boarding in the family and can not speak German very well, said that when she heard people speaking the language fluently, it seemed as if they must be heavenly beings, and not 'of the earth earthy.'

"We hear the lovely Christmas music every evening, sung by groups, who go about the streets, telling the beautiful story of the dear Christ Child. He is much beloved in every German family, and the little ones learn to lisp the name, among the first words they speak.

"Every household is busy preparing for the great event, and a Christmas tree is to be found in every house.

"Since I began writing this the snowflakes have been falling, and a big snow-storm is promised. We are to go this evening to visit the booths and shops, and make our selections for our own Christmas tree, with which we are to surprise our dear friends.

"It was even so, and we started out in spite of the snow, our good Dr. T—— going with us, to help carry the bundles and pilot us safely through the crowd. It was very cold, but we were well wrapped up, and it was rare fun to go from booth to booth, buying here and there some of the curious and also pretty things which were displayed.

"We were so excited that we talked a mixture of English, French, and German; much to the amusement of Dr. T——. He, poor man, was loaded down with a tree and big bundles, and our arms were full, as we emerged in triumph from the last booth we had entered.

"We turned our steps towards our pension, having spent our money, but happy in the thought that we should give pleasure to our friends. Frances lit her wax taper, we said good-night, and climbed the four flights of stairs with our treasures, which we should arrange the next day.

"On the afternoon of that day Mrs. L—— and a party of our girl friends said they should like to borrow our room, which we gladly allowed, and we were politely asked to remain away until called. This we gladly did, for in the adjoining room we were to have our tree.

"Good Dr. T.—— knew the secret and had come to assist us in this plan, while Mrs. L—— had brought her two sons to help her. Frau S—— came in and told us just how to arrange the little tree, and it came out as dainty as one could wish. The boughs were hung with bright balls and colored candles, bonbons, and candy bags, while arranged about it were little gifts as tokens of love to our kind friends.

"The darkness had come before we were done, and just as we lit the candles on our Christmas tree, a call was given for us to enter the other room. As we entered, our surprise was great, for in the centre of the large table stood a beautiful tree, glowing with its lights, and the many brilliant ornaments shining like stars; among the boughs were hung different toys in the shape of all kinds of kitchen utensils used by the Germans; also a poll-parrot swung in its cage; then at the very top was placed the Christ Child, in robes of white. About this tree other presents were placed, and we received many beautiful books, ornaments, pictures, and a dainty little china set of dishes for afternoon teas, with two real gold spoons of the smallest size, which were made of coins. Our good friend Dr. T—— gave these to us.

"Then we opened the door, and our little tree held its head up bravely, with its shining lights. Our friends were entirely surprised and delighted with their gifts. Frau S—— brought in hot coffee, and we feasted on the sweets which had been provided; then played games and told Christmas stories, until the hands of our clock pointed to a late hour.

"Christmas Day dawned bright and clear,

and we ate a fine Christmas dinner with Mrs. L—— and her family.

"A nice letter came from our sweet little Lucia of Laase, asking us to spend the Christmas-tide with them, but we shall stay in Berlin and visit many places of interest which we have not seen. Wishing you again a Merry Christmas and a Happy New Year,

"With love, Pearl."

The vacation time was spent in visiting numerous places: the National Gallery, the Aquarium, Botanical Gardens, and the many picture galleries, various art rooms, and panoramas. So the days passed until New Year's Day came.

A party of young folks had been invited to the hospitable home of Mr. and Mrs. G——, to enjoy an "American dinner" and watch the Old Year out and the New Year in.

A royal good dinner it was, of oyster stew, salmon, potato, and two bouncing turkeys, with cranberry sauce; then a grand plum-pudding, brought to the table with burning brandy on it, mince and apple pies, nuts, raisins, and fruit, with coffee, completed the feast.

Then followed speeches by the host and

some of the older ones, and singing, games, and dancing went on, until the hands of the clock pointed to twelve. All was quiet, waiting for the strokes of the bells to cease; then such a shout arose of "Happy New Year!" from that merry company, that the very walls rang out the joyous sound.

They were happy, indeed, — blessed with beauty, health, and the opportunity to gain so much knowledge in their young days.

The Philharmonic concerts were very enjoyable. As Pearl said, "It would seem very funny to you to see every one eating a lunch between the selections. We regale ourselves with chocolate bread and German sausage, which I quite like, but Frances looks rather doleful as she patiently tries to dispose of her share. As Frances has sent home her account of her average expenses, I will say that my own will be about 279 marks, or $69.75 per month; this will include board, lessons, piano, music, and *sundries.*"

So the weeks vanished, the weather was very cold, so that the warmest of clothing and furs were necessary for comfort. The January and February days came and went, and now March was near at hand.

Pearl was nearing her birthday, when she would be seventeen years old. This was the second birthday away from home; the first had been remembered by kind friends in London, who gave a dinner-party in her honor. Her sister's birthday had been passed in Sassnitz, which Frances thought was a pleasant way to celebrate.

The day came, and about ten o'clock Pearl saw Dr. T—— and his wife coming towards the house; he was carrying a big bundle, which proved to be a lovely basket of flowers, all growing in little flower pots: lily-of-the-valley, hyacinth, and narcissus, placed in a pretty gilded basket. His wife brought a dainty perfume bag and a nice book.

Then Mrs. L—— came, and many others, who all gave as tokens of love fragrant flowers.

The girls were joined by their young friends in the afternoon, and they went shopping to buy "a little treat." Pearl was to choose, and she selected a pot of little fish, like sardines, a roll of cheese, a tumbler of apple jelly, a loaf of English bread, some salmon sausage, and other dainties. Then they went back to the pension and had a feast, passing round the tea in the Christmas tea-service.

As Pearl wrote, "How we did enjoy it, and it was a lovely birthday, for many of my friends thought of me, although I am so far away from home."

About this time it began to be said that the dear old kaiser was ill. From day to day the people waited in Unter den Linden, near the palace, for news of his welfare. One day he would be better, another worse. At last the sad news came that he was dying; then, that the spirit had gone to the Good Father in Heaven. The crown prince was now emperor.

Frances wrote, "I can imagine how you are wondering what we are doing and seeing here in Berlin, in these exciting days, when the whole world, as it were, is plunged in the deepest sorrow on account of the death of the good Kaiser Wilhelm. It is, indeed, a privilege to be here now; and in after years we shall like to remember how the German nation mourned for their beloved kaiser.

"On Friday last came the sad news, and every heart was wrung with pain. The streets were at once flooded with people, who rushed in crowds to Unter den Linden, where the kaiser's palace stands, and in a few hours signs of mourning were everywhere.

"Every house, almost without exception, in the city, was draped in black, and flags of crape were streaming from the house-tops. The people looked very sad, speaking softly, and no laughing was to be heard. All the ladies are clad in the deepest mourning; even the poorer class thus show their sorrow.

"The first time we ventured out in the street people looked at us curiously, for we had worn our same hats and cloaks, so that we felt really uncomfortable. Once, in passing a group of soldiers, they said 'schwatz,' meaning black. The next time we wore black gloves and veils, in token of our sympathy with them.

"The body of the kaiser was placed in the Royal Church, so that the people could go in to see him. We did not attempt to go, for the crowd was so great that it was impossible. The Kaiser Frederick came from San Remo, but so sick that he was unable to speak. This is, indeed, a sad time for Germany.

"Another week gone. Oh! it seems as if the moments were just flying away in almost too great haste. This last week has been a very exciting one. We did not see the kaiser as he lay in state. The crowd was so great that it was hardly safe to try. Frau V——— said she waited from seven in the morning until seven at night before she could enter, but it was a most beautiful sight.

"Early Friday morning, the day of the funeral, crowds of people made their way to Unter den Linden, to see the solemn procession go by. All the houses were deserted, servants and masters alike sharing in this sad occasion. We joined the throng and obtained standing room in the Thiergarten, where we waited three and a half hours in the snow. It was intensely cold, and the only way we kept from freezing was by keeping close together in the crowd, and stamping our feet all the time. It was really dreadful to see such a mass of human beings crowded together, drawn to this spot by a common sorrow. The trees were full of people, perched like birds away up in the tree-tops.

"At last we were rewarded for our long waiting, as the solemn music of the band was heard, and troops of soldiers appeared, looking fine, an honor to their country. We saw them in all their glory that day.

"After the soldiers came the coffin, made of gold and precious stones, which held the remains of the dead hero, and following that the kaiser's war-horse, riderless, led by a masked

man.   Tears came into my eyes as I saw this
faithful animal, which had been so dear to the
old soldier.   Then came the noble kings and
princes, in numberless carriages.

"Much anxiety is felt for the health of the
new emperor, and the people know that they
must soon mourn the loss of this noble man.

"We attended a morning concert given by
Von Bulow.   They gave the 'kaiser march,'
from Wagner, and when the orchestra reached
a certain part, Von Bulow turned to the audience, and, as if stirred by a common impulse,
every person in the audience rose and stood
with bowed head until the music died away.
It was most grand and impressive, such a
tribute to the dead ruler.   All the people were
in mourning, and one could hardly keep back
the tears.

"We are now thinking of our home-coming,
and say we must make good use of our time,
for we wish to get all the knowledge we can to
help us in our life-work.   We are getting a
little tired of German food as a regular diet, as
we have had bread and sausage for seven
months, and we long for some American cooking.

"One evening we had a genuine American

'candy pull,' at the house of our good Dr. T——. Thirty young people were invited. All were expected to work, and it was rare fun. We made twelve different kinds of candy. Then we sang college songs, as usual, which made the Germans open their eyes in wonder. We dined at the house of Mr. G——, and enjoyed the roast beef and the Boston cream-pie, as Mrs. G—— called it, made for our special benefit.

"The Von Bulow concerts are now over, much to our regret, for we have enjoyed the exquisite music so much all the season. Germany is the place to hear good music, for it seems to be a part of the place, and the people seem to thrive on this art. I have enjoyed this privilege as much as Pearl has, even though I am not musical. It has been a great help to her in her chosen work."

So April came, and then May, and still the kaiser was alive, but his death was expected every moment, and any unusual noise seemed the signal that "the kaiser had gone."

During these days of waiting life went on, and the air grew balmy, the sky blue, and the country was again fragrant with the new life. Suddenly the heat became almost unbearable.

To change the scene, a day in the country was planned by the German professor. It was a half-hour's ride from Berlin. When they met at the depot to take the train the professor was not there. Just at the last moment he rushed in, followed by his wife.

After the train was in motion, he exclaimed, "Where are the children? They have been left behind."

"They will be more happy at home," replied his wife.

"Poor dears, we must buy them some bon-bons to make up for thus leaving them," he replied.

The heat was very great, and swarms of mosquitoes beset them as soon as they entered the woods. A young lady, who wore a low-necked dress, was rendered miserable by these creatures, who attacked her vigorously.

Despite these troubles the company was a merry one, and much enjoyed the country air and sights.

Soon after this the girls were met by Frau S——, on coming to breakfast, by "Emperor Frederick is dead!" The cry was taken up all over the world that "Frederick the Noble" had gone to his reward. Again the people of Germany were called upon to mourn, and now the young Emperor William was the head of the German nation.

In May came the day for house-cleaning, and all the German housekeepers were kept busy for some time with these duties.

"Our good Frau S—— is always a neat little housewife, but now every thing must be put out doors for a thorough airing," Pearl said to a friend, who had chanced to call in the midst of the process.

Frances and Pearl had much to do, preparing for the journey homeward, which now seemed almost a reality, as the time flew by.

"Oh! that ocean, it seems so wide to me, when I think of crossing it again," Frances said.

"BERLIN, *June 26th.*

"*Dear Family,*—This is probably the last letter you will receive dated from Berlin. I am afraid it will be a short one, for we are packing, and have many things to do, and numerous calls to make. The heat is intense, and every one who can is planning to again leave Berlin for the summer. Pearl has taken her last lesson of her 'dear professor,' and she really cried when good-bye was said.

"We are to start in three days, with Dr. T—— and his wife to take care of us, and go to London by way of Cologne. We shall make a visit in London, for our many friends there wish to bid us God-speed. Then we shall go to Liverpool and sail for *America*.

"Dear Berlin, how many happy hours we have spent within its gates! Think of us on our homeward way, and pray that we may be kept safe from all harm.

"With best love,

"FRANCES GREY."

.   .   .   .

Two girlish figures stood on the deck of a noble steamer which was nearing the shores of America. All nature, the blue sky, the fresh breeze, the bright sun, and the lovely green country-side seemed to welcome them, and when they were clasped in loving arms the welcome was complete.

It seemed hardly possible that for two years so many miles had divided them from their loved family. They looked the picture of health, with eyes so bright and cheeks so rosy. The joy of going had been great, but the home-coming was even a greater pleasure.

.   .   .   .

We leave them here, happy in their chosen lives, eagerly seeking to lend their aid in every good word and work.